Smells Like Stars

Smells Like Stars

D. Nandi Odhiambo

BOOK*HUG 2018

FIRST EDITION

The production of this book was made possible through the generous assistance of the Canada Council for the Arts and the Ontario Arts Council. Book*hug also acknowledges the support of the Government of Canada through the Canada Book Fund and the Government of Ontario through the Ontario Book Publishing Tax Credit and the Ontario Book Fund.

Book*hug acknowledges the land on which it operates. For thousands of years it has been the traditional land of the Huron-Wendat, the Seneca, and most recently, the Mississaugas of the Credit River. Today, this meeting place is still the home to many Indigenous people from across Turtle Island, and we are grateful to have the opportunity to work on this land.

LIBRARY AND ARCHIVES CANADA CATALOGUING IN PUBLICATION

Odhiambo, David Nandi, 1965–, author
    Smells like stars / D. Nandi Odhiambo. — First edition.

Issued in print and electronic formats.
ISBN 978-1-77166-423-3 (softcover)
ISBN 978-1-77166-424-0 (HTML)
ISBN 978-1-77166-425-7 (PDF)
ISBN 978-1-77166-426-4 (Kindle)

    I. Title.

PS8579.D54S64 2018   C813'.54   C2018-904265-6   C2018-904266-4

PRINTED IN CANADA

For *meine Liebe* Carmen

15 Days to Wedding

<u>6:20 a.m.</u> Lightning reaches down into Ogweyo's Cove like aliens randomly snatching up prey from the *Lebenswelt*,[1] while ticking timepieces separate a ceaseless procession of birthdays, weddings, and funerals that hurtle forward like a train on top of wheels gobbling rail line. Under an awning at the OC Bank of Commerce, Schuld and Woloff wait out an early-morning storm, huddled together in the boomdicrackle of thunder. There's another flicker of light. Wind sweeps away tree branches and dumps them into the thudbump of waves that blather, dismount, and remount several blocks away.

"Here's a question." Schuld tugs at fluffy auburn toppling curls and leans into him. "At what point in a person's life might it not be okay to be a screaming, tight-panted U2 fan?"

"The question, I believe, should not be if at one point it's no longer okay to be a screaming, tight-panted U2 fan," says Woloff, a lanky brother with an ochre circle smeared around his eyes and forming an oval on his chin, and whose long

---

1. The lifeworld (Edmund Husserl)

braids are woven with ochre wool threads. "It should be, is it *ever* okay to be a screaming tight-panted U2 fan?" He adjusts straps on the shoulders of a backpack stuffed with philosophy textbooks before looping an arm, covered from wrist to elbow with bronze bangles, around her.

Above them, a jumbo jet rattles iron girders in the rain-drenched buildings that decorate a cove surrounded by tropical rainforest where slaughtered horses were found tangled among tree roots interlaced with mud. The aircraft floats in troposphere over bucking hills that break into flats of the P.B. & Associates macadamia nut plantation on the east side, and their properties, a slew of beachside vacation rentals surrounded by gangly hotels. The plane hits chop as it passes rock cliffs embedded with steam holes that hiss beside ocean bullying the shoreline. Leaving the island in its wake, the jet stumbles through pockets of turbulence, doddering above tides triggered by a dry run with nuclear warheads detonated in the water hundreds of klicks away. Then it disappears above unmapped depths populated by hatchet fish with ghoulish masklike anglerfish with electric lanterns dangling between bulbous eyeballs.

"My turn," Woloff says. "What was the first big dream you had?"

"To be a Bond girl," she replies. "No, a circus director. You know, I'd wear a hat and gloves, and come out from behind the curtains and introduce the performers. 'Now for the acrobats on unicycles,' and afterwards say stuff like, 'Yes. Yes. Thank you. Thank you, Tracy. You're an inspiration.'"

"I wanted to be Akumbo Taabo, the one-eared African chess champion," he says.

"He only had one ear?"

"When he finally lost the championship, he got in a duel

with the two-eared challenger at what is known as the Massacre at Wolo River."

"You're kidding?"

"Correct."

Rapid sparks of lightning stretch across the sky, followed by rolls of thunder. Schuld and Woloff burrow into each other's arms. Rain kicks up hard, splashing them and pounding cars that have slowed to a crawl on the road.

"You got the next one," Woloff says.

She waits out a grumble of thunder. "Did you and Precious break up?" Schuld asks, referring to Woloff's ex, Precious Namelok, who visits the Cove next week while on a book tour for *Precious: Memoirs of an Insurgent.*

"Yup," he replies. "The last time I saw her, we decided not to make any future plans."

"Sounds like her idea," she says.

"Why?" He brushes away rain from his nose with his forearm.

Lately, Woloff has been texting a lot with her, and it makes Schuld nervous. "Because of all your schedules and writing everything down in calendars," she replies. "You can't live without structure."

"We basically made the decision together to call it quits when I left," he says.

"Basically? Like more or less?"

"No," he says. "Definitively."

Once the storm eases up, they step around puddles and over fallen tree branches on the sidewalk of Krion Street. Time bifurcates future and past in palm fronds that lift, drop, and lift beside them. How much of what they're making together is bound up in what they've left behind? Is it enough that they love each other? Is it? They hold on to tips of fingers while red jungle fowl wander in front of them along the cropped hedges of a gentrified hood planted by the invisible hand of the market. They pass toppled election signs of Governor Ostheim, her grandfather, and emerge at Denturra Beach Park, where a hermit lies on sand swaddled in pea-green tarp, unable to remember the category of species he belongs to. Around him, the trickle-trackle of wind drags garbage bags into water, carrying them on waves toward the mossy underbellies of anchored warships.

"It's over, huh?" Schuld says.

"Done!" Woloff replies. "*Anakwisha.*"[1]

A church bell clangs on the hour, and a startled seagull flies away from the cathedral's dome with a small fish in its beak. Watching out for trouble, they detour at a bridge where, on other nights, fisherfolk hang lanterns over the chrome railing, their lines dangling among rusty iron columns that support their weight. Sharking left, they enter the market plaza, where shoppers stalk the turf of old money. The breeze wheezes through wheels of abandoned shopping carts next to a courtyard of yakking folk, bandying off the cuff at a burly click of cash registers. These phantoms mill around a fountain filled with pennies they've thrown in with a wish for forward motion into the days predicted in their childhoods. Optimistic. Positive. Similar. Jacked on stimulants. They've willed their bodies to brighter days. Some have taken up the management of small businesses started by grandparents when the neighbourhood was a handful of buildings surrounded by acres of guinea grass. Others have taken their degrees or certificates to totter after sums of money calculated from the stories of those who succeeded

---

1. It's over.

10

by the time they were thirty. A sizable number have taken tales about rejecting expectations into the company of those who'll listen. These ones huddle around drinks and discuss those who have chosen to be busy, in the surrounding offices, accumulating the things they won't be able to take beyond the grave. And amid it all, Schuld and Woloff duck down a flight of steps before following a dangle of custard lights strung along the curve of a road that leads west to Mrs. Lill's convenience store.

"The 19 is coming." Schuld points to the end of the block, where a bus drives toward them. "You'll make it on time if you run for the bus stop."

"I'm walking you to the store."

"It's fine," she says. "You'll be late if you wait for the next one."

"Is it fine?"

"Yes," she replies.

"Really?"

"Laterz," she says.

"Stay safe," Woloff replies.

They kiss before Schuld watches Woloff sprint, bangles clanking, across the street through a steady uptick of grinding axles. His orange neon runners splash in puddles of rainwater before he accelerates along the sidewalk, carrying his backpack in one hand. As he dashes for the bus stop, worry turns cartwheels in her limbs and obstinately parks beneath her chest plate.

She passes a construction crew labouring on the corner, backed by election-poster-covered hoarding, and is made self-conscious about the length of her jean skirt. She crosses Florence Street to the west side and passes hustling sex workers. Gone are the fishnet stockings and stiletto heels.

In come the ginger dress tops and sandals speckled with rhinestones. They lean into the windows of cars that slow at stoplights, drizzling flies, and barter with customers over their value.

* * *

7:29 a.m. Standing in the doorway to her corner store, Mrs. Lill wears turquoise leotards, her platinum pink hair snug in a matching pink sweatband. She cradles Falafel, her yapping Pomeranian, under an arm.

"Make sure you unpack the canned goods onto the shelves," she says, petting her dog on the head.

"I'm on it," Schuld replies.

"I'm gonna get in some cardio this morning," Mrs. Lill says. "The spin class is a killer, but the instructor's easy on the eyes." She adjusts a name tag on Falafel's crocodile-skin collar. "Then it's off for drinks with the girls. Susan's youngest had her first Tooth Fairy experience, and she's bringing pics. I know, right? Adorable!"

Schuld nods.

"Be doubly sure to lock the back door," she continues. "Falafel will be on his own upstairs, poor dear, and I don't want anyone getting into the apartment through the side entrance."

"Done."

She hands Schuld her dog, along with a bundle of keys, before she kisses him on the head. "Check in on him from time to time and make sure he has enough water. Sweetie sometimes likes to spill it on the floor." She scratches Falafel between the eyes. "And don't hesitate to call me if there's a problem."

"Laterz," Schuld replies.

She makes her way with Falafel in her arms to the back of the store as he wriggles and snarls against her chest. He squirms and bares teeth before biting into her shoulder. "*Scheiße!*"[1] She drops him to the floor, and he runs down aisle 2. "Falafel!" The pooch jumps onto a shelf and chews through the plastic wrapping on a loaf of bread. "Quit fucking around." Schuld tosses her suede jacket over his head, picks up the squirming bundle, and hurries with it up the back stairs to Mrs. Lill's apartment. She throws Falafel inside and slams the door shut behind her to frenzied barking.

While Schuld works the cash register, pain spasms at a flap of skin in her shoulder bandaged with supplies from aisle 3. Customers come in and stock up on items to get them through their day, their smiles pinched from hauling around mental gunk and from acting the opposite of what they feel. She runs up their bills and packs their junk—their cigarettes and their deodorant, their caffeinated drinks and toilet paper—into plastic bags they sometimes forget to take with them. They jostle across a whirl of surfaces, extracting a "Good day" as she thinks of tall steel beams that hold up the city, and of big cranes that swivel on top of them and cart around granite blocks, their floodlights beaming down, nipping at bumpers on the highway.

Talk is difficult. Borrowed words complicate at frisky speeds.

"Are you going to watch the comet Monday night?" a chestnut blonde with an umbrella asks.

---

1. Shit!

"No doubt," Schuld replies. "You?"

"Hellooo," she says. "It's been a thousand years since it was last in our inner solar system. I'm stoked."

"My boyfriend and I are gonna watch it through an astronomer's telescope," Schuld says. "We should be able to see it real close."

"I love it," the blonde replies. "Love. It."

As a parade of talkers chatter past, Schuld struggles to remember where pauses for a breath are supposed to be in her sentences.

"Do you have any Marlboros?" asks a bear of a man with toilet paper stuck to his chin.

Words twirl in and out of her ears. "ID," she replies.

"I'm thirty-fuckin'-six," he says.

She tries not to wince. "I still need to see something with your birthdate," she replies.

He reaches into a wallet and slides a driver's licence across the counter. "Happy?"

Schuld glances at it and gives it back. "Sorry. I have to ask," she says.

"Fuckwit," he mumbles.

At a lull in customer traffic, she crouches over to recover. Then she lines shelves with wax paper and unloads cans of baked beans from wooden crates. Upstairs, Falafel howls, and the racket echoes doubly in her ears.

On her return to the cash register, she sees Pearl, a regular with a tat of a spiderweb on her neck, place goods onto the counter.

"I brought a recycling bag," she says.

"That's a five-cent rebate," Schuld replies.

Pearl points at Schuld's shoulder. "It's bleeding."

Schuld looks down at blood blooming on her white blouse.

"Oh, that," she laughs. "It looks worse than it is." She gestures toward a noise on the second floor. "I got bitten by the store owner's dog."

"You need to have it looked at," Pearl replies.

"I'm good," Schuld says.

"You need to get a tetanus shot."

"Nah, I'm fine," she says.

There's no sticker price on a can of peas, so Schuld checks an itemized list, delirious with the bounce of code.

"Did you hear about the three horses dumped in the rainforest?" Pearl asks.

"Yup."

"One of them belonged to the friend of a friend."

"Oh." Schuld swipes a credit card at the machine. "Do you want cash back?"

"No," Pearl replies.

"Press 'No' on the screen."

"Where is that?"

Schuld does it for her. Then she waits for the receipt to appear before handing it to the customer. "I'm really sorry to hear about your friend's horse."

"Friend of a friend." Pearl points again. "Don't forget to have that shoulder looked at."

As her shift passes, Schuld watches customers collect objects that make up their milieu. Toothpaste. A comb. Body lotion. Laundry detergent. Ketchup. All the things within easy reach that make the days possible. The upbeat appear, and their happiness pokes at her. If only she could sleep more than a couple of hours at night, she'd be able to remember what story she's in.

Mr. Erdrick, with a new moustache, pushes a pile of men's mags across the counter.

"Long time no see," Schuld says, distracted by Falafel's barking.

"Did that woman say horses are being dumped in the rainforest?" he asks.

"*Ja.*"[1]

"Never happened!" he says. "That's one of those hoaxes circulating on the internet. I hate it when people rush to judgment before they have all the facts. Food for thought, maybe she should get her head out of her ass long enough to do research. You can't go around believing any old thing that pops up online."

All day people like Mr. Erdrick sell Schuld on their facts. When they aren't met with agreement, they pout in silence or threaten to revoke their friendliness. She doesn't know how to dislodge from the clusterfuck. If she could, she'd lock up the store for the rest of her shift, hide under the cash register, postpone the inevitability of her own death, and think of days when the dimensions of a market-driven matrix no longer measured the contents of a person's character.

* * *

5:46 p.m. Late-sunset yellow dissolves into dark grey over Ka'alipo Beach, a sharp drop from the sand cliffs where palm fronds waggle their forelimbs to phalanges. In a deserted enclave, Schuld lies next to Woloff beneath a coconut tree, entwined in a hammock. The outline of bones protrudes from his pitch-black skin at various hinge points, and as she touches a jut at his clavicle with milky-white fingers, her agitation falls away.

---

1. Yes.

Woloff slides a box of assorted Swiss chocolates toward her. "Good luck with the exhibit." She'll be showing her latest artwork in five days at sHipley Art Gallery, a place where she rents a studio.

"*Danke schön,*"[1] she replies.

"*Bitte schön,*"[2] he replies.

She pecks him on the mouth, rips open plastic packaging, and bites small chunks into a random selection to find the ones filled with nougat.

His cell dings.

"Precious?" Schuld asks.

"Might be work," he replies.

"Check," she says.

"*Baadaye,*"[3] he replies, turning off his phone.

"What's going on with the two of you?" she asks.

"*Hakuna kitu.*[4] Why?"

"She mentioned you in her book."

"Oh, that," he replies. "It's short. Nothing special."

"And you're kinda chummy," she says. "Messaging. Using emoticons."

"That's cause we're kinda chums," Woloff replies, twisting a braid.

"So, you're not still hung up on her?"

"Hells no!" he replies. "Like I said earlier, that's over. Squashed."

The hammock swings in a kick of breeze.

"Got any rolling paper?" Schuld asks.

---

1. Thank you very much.
2. You're welcome.
3. Later on.
4. There isn't a thing.

Woloff flings one into her hands.

"*Asante sana,*"[1] she says.

Woloff rubs the knee he re-injured after putting in weeks of heavy mileage on the roads. He's got one year of eligibility left at Ogweyo's Cove U, and he'd been working on developing his stamina to get through qualifying rounds in the 1,500 at NCAAs. "I'm sick of training in the water." He slaps away at mosquitoes. "Today I did some paddleboarding near a set of waves about half a kilometre from shore. I was bushed from running knee lifts in the shore break, so I wasn't paying attention when a shark's fin broke the surface of the water."

"Dang!" Schuld says.

"The last thing I saw was its tail before I toppled into a surge of waves. When I opened my eyes, I was sinking beneath the surface. I kicked my legs to propel upward, until my head poked out of the water. The brightness blinded me. I didn't know where the fuck the shark was, and my board bobbled beside my head. So I climbed on, clawed my arms in the water, and kicked for the distant sand cliffs. I counted to stop myself from thinking. And as I got closer to shore, I noticed fins swooping in the water around me. Real close. A whole bunch of them." His eyes brighten. "Turtles. They were turtles, and they kept me company until I finally got to shore. Bananas, huh?"

Schuld tugs at tangles in his beard as chittering seagulls circle above their heads. "Are you okay?"

"Ain't nothin but a G thang," Woloff replies, smiling wide.

The pain from Falafel's bite pollutes her brain, and a sliver of irritation enters her neurotransmitters. "Don't do that!" Schuld snaps.

---

1. Thank you very much.

"What?"

"Front."

"Is this about Precious?" Woloff asks.

Schuld calculates the cost of saying nothing. "You say you're just friends," she replies. "But how is that possible? You were together for years."

Woloff pulls her down in the hammock sling beside him, careful to avoid bumping into her injured shoulder. "You got bitten by a dog named Falafel."

"You're changing the subject."

Woloff touches a hint of pubic hair that sticks out at the waistline of her jean skirt.

"I'm not interested in anyone else." He slides his hand under the elastic of her underwear (much like he did that first time beneath a canopy of rainbow trees) and drapes a leg over her thigh. "I'm with you." He kisses her lips, pressing his flesh close to hers. Schuld's fingers sidle in his chest hair before she clamps tight around his nipple, her tongue flickering in his mouth like a butane flame.

She smells of dank heat as he enters her. Then their hips move together, slow at first, until they break like banjos speeding through bluegrass.

Afterwards, they curl in the sling and doze off in a trade wind sweeping sand through the clamour of an ambulance siren.

* * *

11:55 p.m. Distant suns may no longer exist as they walk to Café Hashim's. Traces of lamplight disappear in the dark roots of Schuld's glimmering auburn mane, and she notices her leather boots are scuffed with yellow paint. On Filmore

19

Avenue, they tumble into white soapstone light glancing indifferently from untidy rows of storm drains. Surrounded by office buildings that surrender their facades to breeze, they halt in a nook hidden by a garbage bin to pass around the herb that makes late-night crawlers stagger anonymously into canals. Toot, toot, go car horns. And they smash discarded bottles against a wall drowning in ivy before they totter around a corner and duck into the café.

Beneath saturnine art, doughnuts are glazed, coffee is topped up for free, and they sit opposite one another, sipping caffeine to stay awake. The comet is coming, so they speculate about the cosmos, and about scrambling through to the other side of a wormhole to stare at another galaxy in the multiverse—another trillion galaxies to explore for a place to start again, and build cities, or populate continents.

Schuld stubs a cigarette into a saucer that swims with caffeinated dregs and then tries to say everything that might be important for Woloff to know—she likes a coffee before she goes to bed. Her *papi* was an organic-toothpaste tycoon who left the family to start a life with a woman who owned a chain of boutiques selling children's clothes. They've retired and travel half the year in a Winnebago to national parks across North America. Now her *mutti* is getting remarried to the son of a plantation owner, and Schuld hates that she was pressured to be the ring bearer. "It seemed unfair to make me choose between her happiness and participating in a bogus paradigm that has failed her so miserably." Did she mention she wishes to live in a home with a garden full of pale-blue hydrangeas? Huge ones. In bloom one day and wilting the next, a constant reminder to her of impermanence and the pressure she feels to wring the bejeepers out of each and every moment.

She squinches her brow in embarrassment, and Woloff reaches for her hand.

Now it's his turn to say what is important for Schuld to know. He waits to make sure she's finished before he begins his list. He prefers to sleep with a hall light on. His mother died while giving birth to him, and when Woloff was five his father, a mercenary, was killed in conflict with government soldiers near the border. He was brought up by his uncle Phineas, a car mechanic with a PhD in philosophy. Phineas later became his coach in Africa. Thus, his major in philosophy and his track scholarship. He hasn't been as good a runner as he was his freshman year at OCU, and he's lost sponsors because of it. His university coach felt sorry for him and got him work, through a church, taking care of Rick Sunderland, a sixteen-year-old with cerebral palsy. He took the job because he couldn't tell him he was fine for money from selling weed. Shrooms. Some hash now and then.

"I'm a medicine man," he says. "A bit like Namunyak, the witch doctor."

"Is that someone else you've made up?"

"No, no, Namunyak is for real," he replies. "Whenever I got sick, she was the person I went to."

"Like your family doctor?"

"For fevers. Broken bones. The works. She'd use plants she grew in a small garden and slaughter animals of various sizes, depending on the illness."

"Healing people! That's what you think you're doing?"

"Fersurely," he replies.

As the couple choose how they want to be imagined, they reach across the table to trace fingers in one another's palms. Around them, the sober, whom they good-naturedly detest, trickle out of the café to go home to hibernate. Dull greys illuminate the windowpanes, and it's well after five in the morning before Woloff and Schuld make their way outside to stand at a winking orange traffic light in front of a poster of Colin Riverdale, the thirty-seven-year-old challenger for governor in the upcoming election.

"When do you get your motorbike back from the garage?"

"God knows," he says. "They're ordering parts."

"I miss riding around on it."

"You sure you don't want me to walk you home?" Woloff asks.

"I'm good," she replies.

A couple falls out of an awning-covered door before they stumble toward a parked car.

Schuld pulls closer.

"It's really no problem," Woloff says.

"Go!" she insists. "My place is three blocks away. I'm good."

"Yeah?"

"*Natürlich.*"[1]

They hug before she watches him run across the road and disappear into a city full of vehicles that morph, on the creased horizon, into distant points of shuddering headlights.

* * *

5:49 a.m. Schuld walks along the canal in the prick of lamplight, and up ahead, a shaggy-maned man sits on a wall, staring at black water, trying to find a suitable name for his particular sadness. Farther along, a couple emerges from the

---

1. Naturally.

gaggle of thirty-floor high-rises to walk a golden retriever. As the woman tugs on the dog's leash, they both drown in the itchy fabric of baggy sweaters. Separated by a dull awareness of their intractable differences, they silently continue on their ritualistic stroll before the early-morning talk shows.

Schuld looks down at the cobblestones beneath her feet and beelines for the water fountain.

A crow flutters from a porcelain basin.

"I wouldn't drink out of that if I were you," a man with a blue cap says, pointing to his friend. "He had one too many beers last night."

"It was the sushi, bro," the other one replies. "Believe me."

Schuld stares at a bowl filled with chunky clots of pasta. "Laterz," she says to them, covering her nose.

She turns onto a side street where a black cat slinks through the wheels of parked cars. Salt cakes her skin from a dip in the ocean, and the scent of Woloff's cologne remains in her nose.

"Hey, Red. Wait up!" It's one of the men from the fountain. "Do ya know where we can get some action in this shithole?"

Schuld fixates on the traffic light.

"We're on vacation," his pal with an LA Dodgers cap says. "But there's fuck all to do here."

Schuld hurries into the intersection, her heart beating wildly in her chest.

"What's with the stick up your ass?" the first one says.

"Holy mother of Christ," the other one adds. "Are you a dude?"

Schuld crosses onto the sidewalk.

One of them grabs her arm and spins her around. She tries to pry fingers loose, but the grip tightens. Schuld swings at him with her free hand, clipping the bridge of his nose with her ring. He staggers backwards, cradling his face in his hands. A siren sounds nearby. The man in the blue cap tackles her, and they both fall hard to the sidewalk. Before she can reorient herself, the other one pins her to the ground by the arms. A foot painfully crushes her right hand, a knee digs into her rib cage, a hand clamps over her mouth, and she feels them lift up her skirt.

"He's got a dick."

"Fuck!"

Schuld squirms until they push her back into the intersection and run down the sidewalk laughing. Then she sits up, straightening her skirt, and gets to her feet, ransacked.

14 Days to Wedding

<u>12:03 a.m.</u> In a night delinquent with ivory moon, P. J. Banner Jr. slumps alone on his couch in the living room of his one-bedroom apartment in Aspen Towers. He spent the better part of the night with his fiancée, Kerstin Ostheim, and they finally made seating arrangements for the wedding reception. Kerstin's parents are divorced, and it took a long call to her mother before they got the go-ahead to seat them both at the table of honour. Now Kerstin is back at her place, working on a deadline for an article, and P.J. unwinds watching a repeat broadcast of ladies' figure skating on the Grand Prix circuit. Tonight in the short program, a spunky Romanian is a hipster cowgirl. Next up, the American national champion falls on landing a Salchow, and afterwards puts on a brave face while she clutches a bouquet of flowers next to her coach as they wait in the green room for her scores. The favourite, a Japanese skater in flouncy white, is flawless in her execution. However, while the announcers enjoy her technique, they feel she lacks the energy of the American and the spunkiness of the Romanian.

At the commercial break, P.J. writes down a reminder of a

reminder from Kerstin to call the wedding planner to make sure the tablecloths, curtains, and flowers are all pale blue. Then he goes to the fridge to get a root beer and grabs a blanket from the bedroom before stretching out under it on the couch in time for a profile of the two-time Olympic silver medalist. As the Olympian tugs on the teats of a goat on her parents' farm near Düsseldorf, describing the deliciousness of its milk, he thinks about giving notice tomorrow to the landlord of the apartment his father's money has paid for. He's ready for his new life to begin. The timing couldn't be better. The future is infinite with the possible. He's making a small profit on his own photography business, one that's reaping benefits from changes he's made using recently acquired knowledge of the industry's best practices. He's put up a website with a snazzy splash page. He has a punchy slogan, "Trust us with your treasured moments." He has a presence on Instagram, Pinterest, and Twitter he feeds daily with new content. Customer traffic has been up in the last couple of months, so pretty soon he'll be able to hire a team that will get P.J.'s Photo Lab permanently in the win column.

After their honeymoon in Bali, Kerstin and P.J. plan to move into his pop's vacant beachside property in the gated community of Granger's Grove. It's perfection. The deck looking out onto shore breaks and swells. The sunrises. The works. They'll no longer live next to Kutama Point, with its streets littered with discarded syringes. All he needs to do is find the right time to ask his father.

*　*　*

5:07 a.m. P.J. sleeps and dreams of the exposed part of Kerstin's belly, the one between the hem of her low-cut T-shirt and her gargantuan belt buckle. It's vanilla like soy milk, and pristine like an ivory tusk cleaned for sale on the black market. On a star-spangled night at Ka'alipo Beach, they skinny-dip in crashing surf that shifts in iotas, milli-inched neuron by milli-inched neuron. Three freckles run in a vertical line above her left hip, her frosty hair tight in a bun tugged back over her ears. As they swim toward deep water, she transforms into a mizzen, a white mast, and badgered by trade winds that rock and bop the water, they're swept out to sea.

When he wakes up, pressure pushes against his third rib, his breath is crooked in his esophagus, and it's difficult to swallow. Gathering himself, he steps out onto the balcony to stare down at rowing oars that dip and rip the surface of black water in the Tomi Canal. Sobriety was supposed to make his life better. Instead, he has been making mistakes. Yesterday, he cancelled a meeting with his father because of uncontrollable trembling in his hands—more evidence that he's a long way from a finer version of himself. He's forty-three. He has to do better, but all he wants is to stop being a copy of his father measuring the productivity of his days like a manager going through receipts.

He grips the bannister with both hands and leans forward into a gust of wind.

* * *

1:22 p.m. Dapper and styling in a charcoal slim-fit suit, P.J. leans across a desk to shake the hand of Adrian, the super. "Thanks," he says, staring behind the man's head at a picture of his wife, two older men, and three grandkids. All of them wear white judo uniforms with black belts that match their hair.

"Two weeks," Adrian replies. "No extensions. I have to paint the place and change the carpet."

They're interrupted by Gee, a surf instructor from the second floor. "I'll tell the police, Adrian." He grew up on the island, did various stints with the army at bases all over the Mideast, and, depending on the day you catch him, he may tell stories about his friends in the veterans hospital (where they've been fitted with prosthetic limbs). "I have proof."

"You have one week to get out." Adrian raises a finger. "Exactly one week to fuck off."

"I have photos of customers on the second floor."

"In seven days, I'll change your locks." Adrian picks up the phone receiver.

"I know your girls use those apartments," Gee says.

"Seven days, Gee."

P.J. excuses himself and hastens out the front door, down steps, and out onto a street that bounces with the excrescence of shiny motor vehicles. Then he walks on the edge of the canal where bread-crumb-filching pigeons mill around the fella from apartment 208, who sits cross-legged on a patch of grass, talking to the bird kingdom.

* * *

1:53 p.m. On the shoulder of Dollins Street, P.J. coaxes out the reason for Kerstin's curses—her key's on the kitchen table beside a pot of steeping tea.

"What happened to your jacket?" she asks, pointing to a mustard splotch on his sleeve.

"Life," P.J. replies.

A fly drops from on high to land on Kerstin's chin. "Life happened to your jacket," she says.

"And lunch," P.J. replies.

"Let's try that again," Kerstin says.

"What?" P.J. replies.

"Come here." Her nose wrinkles, lifting a range of dunes that pullulate at the flats of her brow. "We can say hello better than that."

"Happy birthday," he says.

In her arms, there's a familiar wispiness. Brittle. Barely there, like the streaky clouds in paintings she once showed him bundled in the corner of her loft. However, he's uncertain whether to trust the decisions he makes because of wisps, and flickering lightness, and an expanse of giddy feeling. He gingerly disentangles from her, stands back, and mutters about a dinner reservation at a place with tiki torches. "You'll love it."

She does a quick calculation in her head. "If I don't get back into mine, I'm not going anywhere," she says.

"I'll call a locksmith," P.J. replies, flipping open his cell.

It's been six months since they met on a dating website. He saw a profile pic of her squeezing a cantaloupe in the supermarket, forgot to calculate risks, and sent her a message about the outrageously high cost of imported fruit. They went out for coffee with the understanding that neither one was obligated to stick around, and they stayed for three hours, talking about their guilty pleasure in watching *Switcher*, the Nielsen-ratings topper broadcast on Thursday nights. Now they're getting hitched.

After he arranges a visit from the locksmith, P.J. tells her his good news. "I gave notice on my apartment," he says.

"For real?" she asks.

"Yup," he says. "I can't live in a place with a prostitution ring."

She punches him in the shoulder. "What about the lease?"

"I can keep the damage deposit if I'm out in two weeks."

"We're doing this?" she says.

* * *

<u>2:40 p.m.</u> It's in the mid-nineties, no wind. On the bed in her rented house, Kerstin sits propped on large cushions against the wall while P.J. takes pictures of her from a variety of distances with his new point-and-shoot camera. Jacked on caffeine, Kerstin speed-reads a semi-destroyed copy of William Strunk Jr.'s *Elements of Style*. As a journalist, she stays on top of her syntax by scanning half a page at a go. A snapshot. A licked finger. A turned page. And again, her head moves slightly up, then down. Blinkblink. Another lick of the finger. Then another turned page.

P.J.'s subject wears a primrose blouse and orange men's boxer briefs. Her skin's densely freckled at her arms, all over legs, on hands, and speckled in an upside-down triangle at a flushed neckline. As the obtrusive eye of the camera commits her to film, there's evidence of sharp collarbones, and a frosty tangle of hair contrasted by a shade of kohl discolouring around her eyes. Her lips are a glossy Zinfandel red, and this sets P.J. off on an associative trek through a profusion of pink at knuckles, and kneecaps, and the soles of her feet. As he snaps close-ups, he wants to wrestle with her for bottomless quiet in a field of purple lupines full of butterflies drunk on purpure.

She puts down her book. "That's enough birthday photos," she says.

"Just a couple more?" he asks.

"How about a game of chess instead?" she replies.

"It's your day," he says, placing the camera into a leather case on top a dresser.

They break out the board and sit on the bed while a ceiling fan heaps cool air onto them.

"Schuld didn't stay here last night," Kerstin says about her nineteen-year-old daughter. "She's been at Woloff's all week."

"I thought you liked him."

"I do," she replies. "He's just so..."

"Out there?"

"Polite," she says.

"Isn't that a good thing?" he asks.

"I wish I knew him better," she replies.

P.J.'s phone rings, and he excuses himself to talk to the wedding photographer. They have a shoot with the wedding party in an inlet on Ka'alipo Beach, and there's been a cancellation with the small crew. Fortunately, P.J. has the number for an assistant he uses.

"Disaster averted," he says to Kerstin.

"Mutter is looking for a hotel that has an exercise room with free weights, not machines." She checks her phone for another message. "I told her we have plenty of room for her, but she insists on free weights for her new morning routine." She turns it off and puts it in a handbag. "I'll get back to her later. No more interruptions. It's my birthday."

"Chess?" P.J. asks. "Are you sure this is what you want to do?"

"Natürlich." She reaches across the board to squeeze his arm. "It's nice and low-key. I'm done for the day with anything that requires work."

They're getting along, and as such, the state of their union prior to the upcoming wedding is strong. They've been trying

31

to stay ahead of the big tasks. They've sent out invitations with pale-blue paper and gold-embroidered text. They've set up the gift registry on a site with a couple shot, P.J's handiwork, prominently featured above Kerstin's personalized welcome. Of late, it's been gluten-free-cake tastings, clothes fittings, and the finalizing of arrangements for the church service. Their vows still need to be written and the playlist for the DJ put together, but the escalating pressure hasn't been a source of tension between them.

"P.J.," she says.

"Kerstin," he replies.

"*Ich liebe dich.*"[1]

"*Ich liebe dich auch.*"[2]

He becomes her understudy who learns from a mistake with his pawn and has to puzzle his way out of her aggressive opening that he doesn't yet know how to mollify with his knights. She develops her pieces, freeing up her bishops to attack the left flank, and soon his king is trapped before he's able to castle.

What does he know about her?

She likes to sleep with sheets, no blankets.

She takes half an hour to wake up in the morning, covers her head with sheets, lies on her stomach, and grumbles.

She eats dark chocolate, drinks coffee made in an espresso maker, and rolls her cigarettes.

She cries when she doesn't have the words to say what she feels.

She's forty-two.

She looks like a different person in her photographs at

---

1. I love you.
2. I love you too.

eighteen than she does at nineteen. In the former she's still a girl with a bowl cut. In the latter, she's travelled through Europe on a Eurail pass and her cheeks have hollowed out.

She eats breakfast for dinner.

Since she was a little girl, she's always wanted to be a character in a book because lives in novels seemed so much more full and meaningful than her own experiences.

"It's almost time to get ready for dinner," Kerstin says.

"Already?"

"We can finish the game later."

She pushes P.J. backwards onto the mattress before clambering onto his legs.

"Are you sure this is how you want to celebrate?" he asks.

She kisses him.

While he kisses her back, his thoughts move away, calculating the extent and reach of another, wholly other, difficult feeling. Kerstin was married for ten years. Therefore, she seems more practised than him at the habits involved in sharing a life. Already she has transformed his own one-bedroom with dried butterfly wings, lilacs, and Post-it notes on the fridge with reminders of phosphate-free dish soaps for him to purchase. She moved the mattress so that when the morning light casts itself aslant through the panel doors, it hits pillows. Scratched pans have been banished for their high levels of aluminum content. She has replaced his sheets with those with a higher thread count. Rags that have served P.J. admirably since the beginning of the second Iraq War have been discarded. In have come laundry detergents manufactured out of the petals of daffodils. And she notices dust everywhere, unlike how it was when he was on his own, a ball of tumbleweed.

The fecundity of apricot shampoo rises from Kerstin's

hair, and her pale-blue sapphire necklace glances against his cheek. She kicks the chessboard off the bed, sending pieces tumbling to the floor. Between the steady chockchock of the whirring fan, he kisses her pink swell of lips. Excitement rises in him like dough. His palm cups the dampened caverns of her heat, her hand encircling his hardened cock. Soon they're twisted pretzels ravenously frigging each other, their breath catching in flats and sharps.

* * *

7.04 p.m. P.J. drives his dented Volkswagen bus through the part of town cleft in the palate of Ogweyo's Cove. His long hair is in a fold-over, and stubble emerges at his chin. As he heads toward the F-3 highway, the heel of his wrist pivots the steering wheel at the end of a straight arm, Vanilla Ice, ice, baby, playing on the radio.

"Do you dream in colour?" P.J. asks, his scuffed camera case sliding around in the back seat.

"Nah, in black and white." Curls spring in loops from her head, covering most of her face. "I add colour after."

"I can never remember which one it is," he says.

"Are you sure going out for dinner is okay?" She checks her messages. "We've already spent a lot on the wedding. I don't need to make a big deal of turning forty-two."

"Yup," he replies.

"Could you be a little less monosyllabic?" she asks, her fingers flickering across a touch screen before she sends a text to her father.

"Monosyllabic?"

She regrets her word choice. "You always say so little." It sounded harsher than she'd intended.

"Always?" He grips the steering wheel with both hands. "Like when?"

"Other than now?" Kerstin puts her cell back into a pale-blue handbag. "Like you can be vague about when you'll talk to your father about renting his beach house."

"We talked about this already," he says.

"I talked," Kerstin replies. "You were—"

"Monosyllabic."

"—not very forthcoming."

"I got it handled, baby," he says. "These things always work out. Pop's got a lot going on right now. I'll talk to him when he's less distracted."

She can't let it go. "You know that sounds like bullshit, right," she replies. "You've been saying there hasn't been a good time to talk for weeks. You just gave notice and my lease expires in a month. We need a commitment from him soon, and all you do is say it will all work out."

"I guess we'll just have to agree to disagree on this one," P.J. says. "I know him. The timing has to be right."

"I disagree to agree." She won't let it go. "What you're saying is bullshit. You were going to see him yesterday. What's happened that suddenly made that conversation so impossible?"

P.J. recollects peeing himself in the van while waiting in traffic on his way to see Pop, turns up the radio, and raises a finger. "I like this part... 'Word to your mother.'"

Kerstin stares out her window at distant buoys that peak like yellow crucifixes from black water. Good Lord! She shouldn't have to push him to deal with this. She bites into her bottom lip and looks at a row of election posters for the governor, her father, on a low wall of whitewashed stone laced with orange flowers.

"I picked up Schuld's meds from the pharmacy today." P.J. reaches into the glove compartment and fishes out a bag with a bottle. "They're the higher dose—"

"Look out!" Kerstin says.

P.J. pumps on brakes and slows as brights bathe a twisted horse lying on the road.

As they creep closer, they see its body is brushed with dust and spackled with flies. A hole at its stomach bubbles over with intestines, and grafts of pink meat, punched clean through with shattered glass, are scattered long ways across the tarmac.

"Stop!" Kerstin says.

"Take 'er easy." P.J. keeps driving. "It's your birthday."

* * *

7.28 p.m. At St. Tropez, P.J. knows the hostess, Celia, and the waiter, Dhrashan, his best friend, from a shack in plantation housing. He went to Rohrman High with the chef, Steve "Flip" Terrell, who relays birthday congratulations to the table with a recommendation to try the pan-seared salmon basted in oyster sauce, *and* gifts "the birthday girl" a bottle of Bordeaux that tastes of smoked wood.

Beneath a watercolour of a green turtle, they're surrounded by patrons with long-sleeve shirts folded neatly at the cuffs. Muzak is heavy on the soprano sax to recalibrate chemistry out of whack while P.J. talks about the importance of mindfulness. "Most people aren't aware how much the brain dictates what happens to them." Candlelight jiggles between them. "It interacts with whatever data it receives. We don't consciously know it, but the information we focus on shapes how we experience." He taps a fork against his plate. "Makes sense, right?"

He hasn't mentioned the horse, nor has he answered her question about why he missed meeting with his father, and Kerstin thinks of his habit of ignoring uncomfortable realities with abstractions that orbit the centre of a thing, defensiveness rearing up on hind legs, poised to crush opposition. She doesn't want to be judgmental, but it's abnormal to her.

Dhrashan interrupts to deliver a basket of warm rolls covered in a napkin with some olive oil and a plate with slabs of butter.

"Enjoy," he says.

"One sec, D," P.J. replies. "Can I ask you a question?"

"Shoot, brah."

"Do you believe we create reality with our minds?"

Kerstin's innards constrict.

"Sure, for some things." Beads of sweat dot his nose and upper lip. "If you visualize them beforehand, why not?"

"See," P.J. says to Kerstin.

She waits for Dhrashan to disappear. "I don't see anything." Sleeplessness makes her irritable. "A lawn chair in your mind isn't going to produce one in reality, no matter how much you visualize it. This doesn't change because you're hopeful of an outcome, and you see a pattern after the fact."

"There are other ways to look at this," he replies.

"Like?"

He lowers his voice. "You need to be careful choosing the ideas you interact with."

A bang of ladles in the kitchen mixes with a roar of chatter from other tables.

She twists a sapphire ring on her index finger. "I need to go back to the horse." Words in her head fly together, then apart. "We saw something horrific. I can't pretend that didn't happen."

P.J. mindfully takes a deep breath.

* * *

10:22 p.m. When they eventually get home, Kerstin phones Eion Skerrit, the senior editor at *Multi-modalZine*. She tells him about the dead horse on the road and suggests there's a connection to the three found in the rainforest the week before.

"By the time we returned to the spot, it was gone," Kerstin says. "And there weren't any traces of blood on the road."

Eion is first and foremost a professional. "Did you at least get a photograph?" he asks.

"We had problems with the flash," Kerstin says.

"Oh, honey! I need more than an anecdote," Eion replies. "Other witnesses. Pictures. An audio file. Video footage. I'll never get the story to pass muster with the editorial team without intersectionality."

It's impossible for Kerstin to understand how Eion's brain thinks like a committee of the like-minded at the *Multi-modalZine*'s office.

"Get me something concrete," Eion continues. "Then we'll see, cupcake."

On hanging up, Kerstin gathers herself by calling Jacquin de los Santos, her maid of honour who suffers acute sleep apnea and wears a CPAP mask attached to a machine.

"Happy birthday, girl," her friend answers. "*Herzlichen Glücken*...whatever."

"Eion's a total prick," Kerstin replies.

"What did he do this time?" Jacquin asks.

"'Cupcake!' 'Honey!' He's too familiar."

"Again?" she asks.

"I've mentioned it a couple of times," Kerstin says. "Then listened to him explain why I shouldn't be offended."

"How was the rest of your birthday?" Jacquin asks.

Kerstin tells her about the horse and P.J.'s tepid reaction. "He can be a bit disengaged," she concludes.

"This is what happens when you roll the dice with some random guy you met on Tinder," Jacquin jokes. "You get cat-fished. I see it all the time."

"You're my maid of honour. Aren't you supposed to talk me into—not out of—my marriage?"

"It won't get better, you know that, right?" Jacquin replies.

Kerstin laughs.

After she disconnects, Kerstin looks in vain for a birthday message from her father, and quickly responds to one from Mutter that asks if it is alright if she does stay with her, after all. Then she knocks on Schuld's bedroom door.

"*Ja*," Schuld says.

"Are you decent?" she asks.

"Come in, *Mutti*," Schuld replies.

Kerstin finds Schuld seated in bed, propped up with pillows, and staring at the screen of her laptop. Her right hand is wrapped in a bandage, and she uses a single finger on her other one to type on the keyboard.

"*Was ist passiert?*"[1] Kerstin says, sitting down at the end of Schuld's bed.

"Skateboarding accident," she replies.

---

1. What happened?

Kerstin puts a hand on Schuld's arm. "You need to be more careful with that thing." She notices the open window and can smell faint traces of weed in the air. "I'm surprised you haven't broken your neck, the way you leap around on it."

Schuld closes the laptop. "How was your birthday dinner?" she asks.

"*Gut, danke,*"[1] Kerstin says.

"*Schön,*"[2] Schuld replies.

Kerstin picks at the corner of Schuld's bandage. "We've seen so little of each other because of the wedding. "That's going to change."

"Sure, Mutti," Schuld says.

"I've got an idea," she says. "We should visit *Urgroßvater*[3] and *Urgroßmutter*[4] at the cemetery on Sunday morning. It's your day off, we haven't been in a while, and we could spend a bit of time together. Woloff could come if you'd like. We could get something to eat afterward."

"I have other shit to do," Schuld replies.

"What could be more important?"

"The exhibit's in a few days," Schuld says. "I need to work at the studio."

"That can wait until the afternoon," Kerstin replies. "I'll drop you off when we're done."

Schuld winces. "Woloff won't be able to make it."

"Ask him first," she replies.

"Sure, Mutti," she says, looking down at her computer screen.

---

1. Fine, thanks.
2. Great.
3. Great-grandfather
4. Great-grandmother

"Well, get back to your blogging." She stands up and kisses her daughter's head. *"Schlaf gut, mein liebes Kind."*[1]

"Herzlichen Glückwunsch zum Geburtstag!"[2] Schuld replies.

Kerstin carts a low-grade headache to her bedroom and lies in the dark, on top of sheets, while the west wind seeps in.

---

1. Sleep well, my lovely child.
2. Happy birthday!

13 Days to Wedding

6:31 a.m. A train with tourists leaves Ogweyo's Cove, spilling carbon monoxide as it unhurriedly climbs up the face of Mount Putnam, past rows of tower mills, until it disappears behind a satellite dish at the summit. It's Saturday morning. Inside, families maxing credit enjoy the perks of the good life with a bird's-eye view of at least three of the cove's more magnificent locales cited on the show's website: M'Toma Falls, Ka'alipo Beach, and the Alto Pyramid on the outskirts of downtown. Descending the peak, the train barrels past ditches where a cult of forty celebrated the arrival of the rapture by swallowing arsenic several summers ago. This story, broken at the time by Kerstin at *Multi-modalZine*, inspires the train bound to crowd the window to get multiple snapshots of the infamous backdrop for later editing on social media posts.

* * *

6:33 a.m. Sweat from humidity sticks to P. J. Banner Sr.'s clothes and burnishes his bald spot. He surveys his plan-

43

tation of damaged crop from the metal platform of a tower mill. He looks at macadamia nut plants infested with stinkbugs that creep among leaves. This latest infestation affects the bottom line at a time when his future in-law, Governor Gary Ostheim, has made a re-election pledge to enforce the expiration of land leased from the state on the east side for ninety-nine years and return it to the Iqba Land Council. He'd lose about ten thousand acres of uninfested plantations in the fertile belt along the coast, and any compensation would be swallowed up by a trade war involving start-ups in emerging Oceanian markets. Competition has brought down the price of macadamia nuts 33 per cent in the past two years, and he can't afford to give up his most viable land. Not now. It'll eat into more than 27 per cent of P.B. & Associates' profit margins, and the cost of doing business will become a challenge with the union's opposition to his latest plan for job cuts and wage freezes.

He angrily heaves a rock out into the field before he strides to the parking lot.

* * *

8:31 a.m. P.J. Sr. sits opposite Governor Ostheim on the sixth floor of the State Legislature surrounded by hardwood panels on the floor, the walls, and the ceiling. The governor's comb-over is dyed black, and the heat causes streaks of black perspiration to pool on the collar of his dress shirt.

"There was no sign of a forced entry into Sonja and Anastasia's home," P.J. Sr. says of the season-ending cliffhanger of *Switcher*. In its thirteenth season, this prime-time stalwart of the Thursday-night lineup has reinvented cable television with a same-sex marriage between a middle-aged interracial couple. Tamala Exeter plays Sonja the business executive, and local actress Rita Oozol received an Emmy nomination for her portrayal of Anastasia, a veterinarian of mixed heritage. "It doesn't take a genius to figure out it's an inside job."

"Nothing involving Sonja's kidnapping showed up on the surveillance tape," Governor Ostheim replies, the state flag gently fluttering on a bronze pole beside him.

"No, it did not," P.J. Sr. says. "But something is a little off with Anastasia. I'm convinced she masterminded the whole thing."

"That's the mystery apparently," Governor Ostheim replies.

P.J. Sr. sips from a cup of oolong tea and adjusts in his leather chair to avoid aggravating a tense spot in his back. He popped Copax Ltd.'s newly improved sleeping aid on his return from his stinkbug-infested plantations and washed it back with a brandy, so he's been buzzing along ever since while trying hard not to forget what he's talking about. His week has been full. There were calls to field from nervous stakeholders, and a press conference where he denied rumours about layoffs. His mind reels with spin, and he struggles to think of another icebreaker to use in this meeting with the governor (despite teaching useful icebreaking techniques in job-skills workshops offered at a discount to employees of the P.B. & Associates family).

"Did my son tell you that I'm pretty good at figuring out plots?" P.J. Sr. asks. "I can always tell how a storyline will end. It's a specialty of mine."

"No," the governor replies. "He hasn't mentioned it."

While P.J. Sr. provides several examples of his unique gift, lifted from the seventh slide of his PowerPoint, available at a link on the home page of the P.B. & Associates website,

Governor Ostheim hopes his future in-law doesn't conflate personal matters with governance and bring up the sticky topic of his plantations on the east side. Since recent spikes in his cholesterol levels put him at a high risk for diabetes, he wants to make sure legislation passes that will cement a legacy as a pragmatist who took excess government out of regulating financial markets (a subject discussed in the unfinished manuscript of his memoirs). However, it's a dance to figure it all out: how does one make history, feel relaxed, work on breathing, and prioritize the medical team's health plan during his run for the mid-term elections?

"Have you been fishing this year?" he finally asks.

"Not yet," P.J. Sr. replies. Will he be misremembered? It's a question he's often asked himself since the day his heart stopped while he took a Skype call with the board of directors in New York. Now he's marked by this experience in the ways he's a little nauseous all the time, uncertain whether a sneeze will kill him. Therefore, he gets to the point in order to maximize the clarity of his purpose in whatever time he has left. "With all due respect. Is there wiggle room in your position on the expiring land leases? It will hit my business hard at a time when, to be honest, unemployment in the state has been up 4 per cent since the first quarter."

"Sadly, no," Governor Ostheim says.

"Your campaign's war chest could always use a generous donation," P.J. Sr. replies. "Through my relationship with the Conglomeration of Banks, we could set up a PAC that would boost your advertising budget."

"I'm running on this issue."

"We're family now."

"It's a matter of principle for me."

"The loss of land won't impact your pocketbook like it

will those of my employees," P.J. Sr. says. "Let's be realistic. Thirty-seven per cent of the state's workforce is dependent on P.B. & Associates to make a living, not the Iqba Land Council. That isn't a demographic you should take for granted." He flushes at the neck. "With my long-standing relationship with the banks, I'm in a position to put you over the finish line in the next election. You'll go out a winner. That will be your legacy." His accelerating heart hammers between his temples. "If not, I'd happily throw my support behind Colin Riverdale."

"I'm not for sale," the governor replies.

"He's at the beginning of his career," P.J. Sr. says. "Smart. Young. Charismatic. Optimistic. Social media savvy. Everything a well-funded campaign would take advantage of."

"I have work to do," Governor Ostheim replies.

P.J. Sr. puts his cup of oolong tea down on the governor's desk and stands a bit too quickly. The room of wood panels spins in his vision, and he has to focus extra-hard to avoid passing out from dizziness. "You just don't have the coalition for an unpopular mandate," he says. He walks, with great caution, to what looks to him like two overlapping door frames.

* * *

1:07 p.m. Matilda, the house cleaner, hears plastic rip in P.J. Sr.'s bathroom, a loud thud, and then a groan. Gixx, the Rottweiler, barks as she finds him wrapped in a torn shower curtain in the tub. She clambers in after him, and props him upright.

Blood oozes from a gash in the back of his skull.

Once she gets him to hold a towel against his head, Matilda

calls an ambulance. Then, as instructed, she splashes cold water into his face to keep her boss's batting eyelids open while Gixx anxiously scratches at the closed bathroom door.

So begin in earnest the medical establishment's miscellaneous tests and drug experiments with P.J. Sr.'s brain. He's hospitalized overnight, and his moods oscillate between optimism and pessimism while Dr. Crnnčević, wearing green scrubs, a sleeveless lycra top, and red Crocs, gets to the bottom of things. "It isn't a stroke." She reads from notes on a clipboard. "You have no broken bones, but you repeat yourself often. So we'll need to run more tests."

"Is it serious?" P.J. Sr. asks.

"It's too early to tell," she replies.

"Is it terminal?"

"Like I said, Mr. Banner, we need to do some tests."

At visiting hours, P.J. sits in a chair at Pop's bedside. His worried father is propped up on pillows, in a hospital gown, purple blood vessels protruding from his ashen arms. "After I go, my body will be bits and pieces, all over the place. Quarks. Entangled electrons. A part of a swirling weather system." Bedsprings squawk beneath him. "It frightens me. I don't like the idea of having no consciousness." He pulls the sheet off his legs and scratches behind a kneecap. "Unless, of course, the universe eternally expands and collapses while we live the exact same life each time it collapses and returns. That way all we ever have is consciousness of the moments we eternally relive."

P.J. can't get himself to put a hand on his father's arm. He's angry that Pop didn't slow down after his recent stroke. He brought this collapse on with his bullheadedness over the land deal. All of this could have been avoided if he hadn't pushed so hard to extend the land leases another ninety-nine years. It's become about not losing and, frankly, it disgusts P.J. That and his hypocrisy. Pop constantly reminds him how hurtful his coke problem and his stay in rehab have been. Fair enough, but he can't take hearing this from a guy who never apologized for cheating on Mama and spent most of his life two sheets to the wind. P.J. grips the sides of his chair, parts of him go missing, and when his father mentions a possible other life in the multiverse, P.J. doesn't know which way in his head to turn. He's at loose ends: concave and curved like a worn saucepan. "You're alive, Pop," he says. "You just have to take 'er easy."

"I want my ashes to be scattered in the ocean." Pop closes his eyes. "I may not have a consciousness, but I'll be recycled material circulating somewhere...swallowed by a fish eaten by a bird that gets served at supper to a human being. Perhaps."

P.J. remembers him talking about the dead recycled as food once before. He was a boy living in the plantation estate near the tower mills on Mount Putnam. That morning it poured with rain. So he huddled on the sofa beside Mama in the room with the tilting bookcase, reading out words from Pop's books. Big words. Mouthfuls he couldn't say out loud without muscles acting like jackasses in his throat.

"On-slaw-gt," he said.

"Onslaught," she replied, her cotton dress brushing against his forearm.

When the phone rang, she was quick to pick up. As she listened in silence, her brow buckled deep with furrows before she returned the phone to its cradle. "Your Pop's going to be late again." She looped an arm around P.J.'s shoulder and held him close while he worried she'd cry. "I should have listened to Mama. She said before I got married, think of a man like Apna Ki'ikak, the son of the medicine woman. He doesn't just speak—he listens. These are the qualities of a good companion. Instead, I chose your father, someone who rode a motorbike and who only commits to chasing other women and money." Breeze from the window tussled with lifting curtains. "I thought happiness was doing whatever I wanted, but I was wrong." She pulled P.J. hard against her. "Marry someone who knows when to speak and when to listen. Don't be like your mother and do the opposite of what she was told to do."

Once the rain let up, P.J. escaped the sadness in Mama's glazed eyes and spent time with Dhrashan. They sat in the Banners' garage looking through his father's record collection. Pop bought records, not CDs, because he liked the scratchy sound the needle makes in the grooves. And for the longest time P.J. thought Pop said he liked scratchy grooves. So he and Dhrashan looked through the collection for a good scratchy groove.

They checked in a blue trunk.

"Look!" Dhrashan said, holding a cover that had a picture of a bathroom stall.

They waited until P.J.'s mom went out to buy groceries and used the record player in the living room. Sharing headphones, they held their breath and listened to an African-American man.

"Hellooo, motherfuckers!" An audience laughed. "Hellooo, New York!" There was cheering. "What a city! How do all of y'all manage not to lose your shit in this here motherfucker? Shiiit!"

While the motherfucker man talked about how he sat in traffic in a cab for many hours and watched the motherfucking price get high as fuck, the people hooted and hollered.

Then the man said how he was in the airport toilet and made farts and smelly poo. He had no toilet paper and said, "Hey, motherfucker," to other people in the airport toilet, "hey, motherfucker, I got shit all up in my asshole." The crowd howled, and the only reason Dhrashan and P.J. stopped listening was because Mama pulled into the driveway with the car.

They went back to the garage and pulled a cardboard box down from a shelf. Dhrashan took a penknife from his pocket. Snip. He cut string, tossed it to the ground. Then he shoved the blade through Sellotape before slicing open a box full of house paint.

"Wanna paint chickens?" Dhrashan asked.

"Let's do it, motherfucker," P.J. replied.

They took a can of paint, helped themselves to a couple of brushes, and crawled under the fence to track down broods of chickens that followed each other on the grass beside the road. They crouch-walked until they got close to a rusty red cock. Then they chased it around with brushes that dripped white paint. The bird squawked, flapping feathers and darting on the tips of his claws between them.

Neither of them could catch him, so they raced after other roosters that crashed into each other as they flew around them in panic.

"Get the motherfuckers!" Dhrashan howled.

P.J. smiled and began to splatter his friend with paint. Dhrashan yelped and splashed him back.

"What are you doing?" Mama interrupted.

They stopped, covered in paint.

"We're white people," P.J. said.

She crossed her arms. "Go home, Dhrashan." Then she pointed to the gate.

51

P.J. made a run for the house.

For punishment, he had to stay quietly in his room until bath time, and Mama regularly checked to see if he was using the time productively by doing homework. After supper, P.J. sat alone on the front step waiting for Pop to come home. Half an hour passed before his father's yellow Saab bumped into the side of the front gate. The car slowly reversed. Then it lurched forward into the driveway until it sputtered to a standstill in front of the garage.

Pop tilted out of his window. "Hey, buddy." He opened the car door, but fumbled his keys to the driveway. On leaning forward to pick them up, he tumbled out of his seat and fell hard against cement.

P.J. ran over to his father's side and shook his shoulder. "Pop!" he said.

"Hey, son," Pop replied, opening his eyes.

"Are you okay?" P.J. asked.

Pop smelled of boozy fun. "When I die I want to be cremated and scattered at sea," he said. "I'll get recycled by a fish and eaten by a bird that returns to the human body in the supper of a person."

"I'll get Mama."

"No, no," Pop replied. "I'm right as rain."

As he struggled to sit up, Mama joined them.

"Hey, Pineapple," Pop said.

She lifted him up by the crook of his arms and helped him into the house. "Do you know what P.J. did today?" Mama asked.

"I'm sure you'll tell me," he replied.

"He and Dhrashan painted themselves white," she said.

Pop laughed. "That's my little man."

"It's not funny," she replied, depositing him on the couch.

"Can we not do this right now?" Pop said.

"You could at least try to help the boy learn who he is," Mama replied.

"People are people," he said. "There's no need to fill his head with a bunch of racist ideas about our differences."

"That's easy for you to say," she replied. "He painted himself white."

"Jesus Christ!" He placed a palm over his brow to shield himself from the bulb light. "Stop talking like your bloody mother."

"Don't speak about her like that."

"Like what?" he continued. "She's racist toward white people!"

Mama waved P.J. over to her. "Come here, dear!"

"Don't go anywhere, buddy!" Pop said.

P.J.'s heart jumped noisily in his head. Mama was telling him to do this and Pop said to do that, and he was just eyes looking out of a head that couldn't fit words to what was happening to him.

A nurse in green scrubs interrupts from the doorway of Pop's hospital room. "Visiting hours are over in five," she says.

"Already?" Pop asks.

"No exceptions, Mr. Banner," she replies before she steps out of sight.

Time sluices from past to future in milliseconds, and P.J. continues to sit at his father's bedside thinking about how it'd be much simpler if Mama were still alive. Her descendants, the Iqba, discovered the island while navigating oceans on canoes centuries ago and, like them, she'd never have kept score of her acts of kindness for their potential payoff, unlike his father. For Pop, everything's a transaction

53

that binds creditors and debtors in a mutually beneficial system of rewards and punishments. His grandparents arrived with the wave of white entrepreneurs who made a fortune on macadamia nut plantations. Now he owns the majority of private land surrounding Ogweyo's Cove, a collection of residential properties, golf courses, beachside resorts, and plantations.

P.J. stands up. "I'll be back tomorrow."

"Is Matilda taking good care of Gixx?" Pop asks.

"As much as he'll let her."

"I need to check my messages," Pop says. "Can you bring my cellphone with you?"

"We'll first see what the doctor has to say about that."

"I'm swell," he replies.

"We'll talk tomorrow," P.J. says, backing toward the door and away from sadness piled between them multiply. Perhaps the day will come when they'll talk reasonably and understandings between them will be reached. Perhaps.

12 Days to Wedding

<u>8:42 a.m.</u> Schuld rouses to take routes that aren't her own. She blinks, checks for tenderness around the bite in her shoulder, looks over bruises on her thighs, and with great difficultly opens and closes her wounded hand. Once she's awake enough, she moves from her bed to save a fly that bats wings against the inside of the bedroom window. It has thousands of eyes, she's been told, but it cannot see well.

"Sorry," she says.

She opens the window, setting it free. Then she cups a palm over a line of ants that march along the windowsill before she scoots them onto the grass.

No one else is awake. Mutti is in bed with P.J. at the other end of the house, and Schuld doesn't want to see either of them until she manages to feel happier about her day off from work. She feels around the edge of a bruise on her shin while voices spiral around her cranium saying things she hesitates to repeat when watched. What is there to smile about? The assholes that assaulted her have left her less inclined to leave her bedroom to face what awaits her outside.

Talking to her mother about the latest incident won't help

because it only means even more work for her to do and new rules to follow. Fill out a report with the police. Don't go out alone. Come home straight from work. Go see Dr. Philbin, the therapist, for an adjustment in your meds. It will throw her back into the queasiness. The beatings aren't all that there is to her, and she doesn't want to get sidetracked by focusing on them. Instead, she wants to use much of her day making art that acknowledges the weight of existing with others without letting it define her.

Sitting up on her bed with her laptop, she wills a crushing fatigue to lift as she surfs the interwebs.

She clicks on bold fonts and swims among accumulating piles of hyperbolic text for inspiration. She has to find a way forward, one where she isn't playing an expected role that makes her unrecognizable to herself, one that imagines different conditions of possibility within her experience of violence, not as an idea, but by creating an encounter that forces responsible thought in the world beyond her.

After an eternity of clickbait, she notices a trending election thread from her grandfather's opponent.

ColinRiverdale@ColinRiverdale—8m
I don't use SOFT and IMPOTENT to draw attention to Gerhard's name or his old age. Ridiculous!!!

ColinRiverdale@ColinRiverdale—10m
FYI My use of Gerhard instead of Gary isn't an insult. IT'S HIS NAME. GOOGLE IT.

ColinRiverdale@ColinRiverdale—2h
Real talk. Unbelievable. Geriatric Gerhard is SOFT ON CRIME. His closed door meetings with the Iqba Land

Council shows he's IMPOTENT and not UP TO THE TASK. Just saying.

Schuld opens her bedside table drawer and takes out a jade stone ring lying next to a semi-automatic handgun wrapped in a handkerchief. She puts the ring on her middle finger. Then, to avoid the voice in her that speaks to the one that listens, she goes to the bathroom to douse the wound on her shoulder with peroxide, changes the Band-Aid, and returns to her bedroom, without feeling, in order to reblog quotes about death.

* * *

10:01 a.m. Kerstin hurries Schuld out of the house to make sure they get to the cemetery at the predetermined time.

"They expect us at eleven," Kerstin says.

Schuld draws on all her willpower to avoid pointing out that Urgroßvater and Urgroßmutter are both dead.

"Is Woloff coming?" Kerstin asks.

"Ne."

"Did you ask him?"

"Natürlich."

Five minutes later, Schuld sits in the front seat of her mother's red vintage Alfa Romeo in the driveway and waits while Kerstin doubles back to the house to make certain the floors are swept, and the cupboards closed, and the windows shut, and the elements on the stove turned off, and the garbage taken out. Meanwhile, Schuld gets angrier that they'll be fifteen minutes early and end up parked on the street down the block from the cemetery. She likes visits with her great-grandparents, but they aren't a solution to the tension with her mother. In fact, it seems strange to her whenever Kerstin finds ways to bond with her over Urgroßvater's life as a woman living as a man with Urgroßmutter. Yes, they survived a war, moves to two different continents, and a lifetime of secrecy. However, drawing attention to this past only makes things more awkward.

When Kerstin returns to the car, she plops down at the wheel and goes over a mental checklist. "Did you pick up the dry cleaning yesterday?" she asks.

"*Ja*," Schuld replies.

"I didn't see it anywhere."

Silence.

"Schuld!"

"It's in the trunk."

"*Scheiße!*[1] You left the dry-cleaned clothes in the trunk?"

Schuld's eyes prick with heat.

Kerstin gets out of the car, slams the door, and retrieves the clothes in order to put them inside the house. Schuld bristles, recollecting how she watched her parents cling to one another like two people who parachute from an airplane in tandem before growing increasingly entangled the closer the ground approaches. It was nothing like their picture on the mantelpiece taken beside the remains of the Berlin Wall the day Papi told Mutti, "*Ich liebe dich ganz, ganz doll.*"[2] Now Papi is gone, and Mutti obsesses over every decision she makes outside of a narrow range of her routines: her morning teas, her writing, her wedding plans, and her spare time spent endlessly with P.J. in front of the TV.

---

1. Shit!
2. I love you loads and loads.

* * *

12:44 p.m. Outside the front door of the art galleries build-ing, Schuld encounters a frail teen who stands on a planters ledge with dangling earrings that smoke ice. She chews gum and bops to hardcore hip hop that blasts from a deck at her feet. She waits for her man, tatted up with green ink on his legs. He presses buttons on an intercom.

"Yo, Red," the teen says.

"What up?" Schuld replies.

"An associate of mine's on the third floor giving us a place to crash tonight and left his door unlocked," she says. "He ain't in right now, so we needs someone to let us in. Can you hook us up?"

Schuld hasn't rented studio space in the building long and doesn't want to make waves. Rule #3 in the bylaws is clear. Only "leaseholders and guests accompanied by ten-ants in good standing" are allowed in. No exceptions exist for strangers. Even if the Pope himself descended from his bulletproof motorcade and wanted in so as to perform a blessing in the lobby, no dice.

"Can't do it," Schuld replies.

"C'mon, baby girl," she says.

"If you gimme two hundred bucks to cover the fine, I'll let you in," Schuld replies.

"You gonna charge us two hundred to get in?"

"No. I'm saying that I'll get charged two hundred bucks if I let you in," Schuld replies. "So I'll do it if you give me the money upfront." As hardcore hip hop chronicles disembow-elment with pool cues in assorted orifices, Schuld tries to re-explain herself with a confusing reference to the Pope. "In God we trust, all others pay cash," she concludes.

The woman gets in her face, but quickly steps back in disgust. "She a tranny."

Her man steps up and pokes a finger into Schuld's temple. "Cocksucker."

Schuld pushes him away and pulls the semi-automatic from her belt. "Don't fuck with me." She waves it in their faces.

The door behind her swings opens, and Demarion Armstrong reaches out to drag her inside the building by the arm. She struggles to get back outside, fighting to break free of the 7-foot-8 giant's grip. He holds her fast and doesn't let go.

* * *

3:39 p.m. Schuld calibrates her body like it's an engine. Three cigarettes get the corpus callosum humming. Assorted house plays on the iPod. She looks in a mirror. Should her hair fall freely over her shoulders, or would it look better fastened by a clip at the back of her head? She opts for the clip. Set, she walks around a bathtub stained with an accumulation of half a century of rust until an idea occurs.

She fiddles with an elastic band on her wrist. Then focuses on the tub, a hopped-up jumble shot through with gaping holes. Impulsively, she dips one of an assortment of thick brushes into a can of green paint before leaning over and smushing it onto white space.

She thinks of skateboarding in trade winds, and of sun glinting like bits of glittering tinsel from waves. She has a hit of hash, smears more paint from brush to porcelain-enamelled cast iron, whirls from one spot to another, and says, "Fucking eh." Distress piles on, and out comes a whole lotta chaos. She remembers lying on the sidewalk with a broken arm while a bobbling doll shook hips on the front bumper of a parked cab. She stops and tries to listen to the voice that commands her body not to react by responding in expected ways to those who have their certainties about how people (like her) should behave. Enraged. Depressed. Reductive to remain comprehensible. Hectoring to assert the right to exist. Focused on the inevitability of her tragic martyrdom. She wills herself to different possibilities, but it's unclear if fatigue will cooperate. Concentrate harder, the voice tells her, and out tumbles an impression of nights Urgroßvater sits at her bedside when she was Phillip while he says his nightly prayers. She wonders, for a beat, if it is okay that she thinks of herself in the past as the boy who said his nightly prayers with Urgroßvater. Asking for the safekeeping of his family, of course. And for a happy world with no wars, obviously. And he prayed for the hungry children around the globe, asking God for rain for them, and apple strudels for them to have for dessert, and for lots of money so they could have a house with enough bedrooms for everyone. And for several weeks Phillip slipped food from his meals into his pockets, put it in envelopes addressed to the Hungry Children of the Globe, and he walked with Urgroßvater to deposit the letters in the mailbox down the street until the mailman complained about the smell.

Schuld switches to chalk and works until she settles enough so she won't have to lie in bed fighting to be still.

12 Days to Wedding

4:12 a.m. As Woloff listens to bebop on headphones, twisting wool into his dreads, dawn comes and goes, went and came, much like the trains that sped near his home through the surrounding bleach savannah loping with killer bees. Springs from his mattress are difficult against his back, a blizzard of pocket trumpet navigates in his cochlea, and when a stride piano solos over the tip-tap of a hi-hat, a new moon accessorizes the frame of his window, engorged with yellow. He thinks of Precious Namelok. Her Twitter account announced the sale of movie rights for her memoir (on Precious's Facebook page, she shared what was on her mind with a shout-out to a "true inspiration, Eric J." and added a trending GIF of a touchdown celebration that included the stanky leg). In the time he knew her, she never apologized for disappearing for days, doing whatever the fuck. She'd go on raids with insurgents against mercenaries near the border. She'd get in knife fights in bars. It was generally thought among those who knew her that she was doomed to fornicate and die of AIDS, or get stabbed in an alleyway, or be hit by a bullet in a firefight like the venerated list of thuggish

MCs who commanded her loyalty. Now she's on a book tour. Very much alive. And he's with Schuld.

At first light, Woloff tests his left knee as he picks up leg speed through streets of Ogweyo's Cove, a stretch of names he still can't commit to memory. In the early light grey, cocks crow, a reminder of home with its wire chicken hutches and yellow chicks, balls of fur, trotting after their mamas. He goes back to being in the water with a shark and the uncanniness of being escorted by turtles, shuddering at how close he came to being eaten. Apartments hem him into a city of pigeons sitting on corrugated rooftops, the day braced by a smear of orange that flares on the horizon. When he turns into the suburbs, humidity bites his skin, and he can't stop thoughts about yellow weavers flying into caged bars, smacking into steel until they're weak enough to lie down next to one another and die.

Headlights of gas-mobiles blister the morning as he jogs through a crosswalk. Drivers honk horns, and he carefully leaps onto the sidewalk before stepping around lovers who clutch one another by the ass and paint one another's earlobes with spit. As he enters a stretch of road through a line of graffiti-covered stores, Woloff concentrates on briskly moving his feet. His legs are heavy, but his knee feels good. He throws in a hard surge next to chain-link fence, dips left onto a bicycle path, and feels a twinge in his leg. He stops abruptly, and he limps gingerly toward a low retaining wall of grey stone that lines the ash and eroded limestone of Denturra Beach Park.

"Shitshitshit," he says, angry with himself for staying out of the ocean because of fear.

Farther away, children run back and forth, tramping past coconut trees and scuttling across the wet sand in a sliver of another story told by a landscape mined for its potential to produce macadamia nuts, sold locally at twice the price they go for abroad. He massages the back of his knee and tells his mind to be quiet.

It bucks, wriggles free.

As a motherless boy at the home near the shores of Lake Victoria, Woloff slept among billions of galaxies made from crushed diamonds, and finally woke up one morning, infinitely small. He gathered all the things he loved around him. A jar of tadpoles. Bedtime stories of loyal hounds. Bedtime prayers to wish them well. A field of pale-yellow gardenias swarming with pale-blue butterflies. And when it rained, it poured. His father disappeared near the border, his body turning up in the carcass of a vehicle that rusted in a gulley he'd been dumped into. Unable to eat, Woloff huddled at the speed of dark on a straw mat in front of Namunyak, the witch doctor. Spirits hooked in the emaciated thorn bushes while she threaded a knife blade between a rooster's wattle. Tsetse flies suckled Namunyak's dark flesh, and sprinkles of blood pricked their way across fields of sugar cane, blotted red in the dust.

Namunyak held the spasming rooster up to dim starlight. "He has no was." It spattered her with bloodlets. "Only what he becomes."

"What do you advise?" Uncle Phineas asked.

She approached Woloff, who flinched when she placed a bloody hand on his knee. "*Unapaswa kurudia tabia.*"[1]

"He needs his habits?" Uncle Phineas asked.

"Take from the past and steal from the future to make time," she replied.

---

1. You must repeat behaviour.

It was decided that Woloff would move in with his uncle in order for material objects to begin leaving impressions in his head again.

Within a year, fields of maize bowed outside the window of a train that belched diesel as it carried him to a boarding school (with stark rooms and bunk beds and rules maintained with the threat of beatings). Each morning, bees descended from the cool shade of trees while he sat in noisy dining halls, unable to swallow food boiled in metal vats and served by those who lived in nearby villages. Everywhere he looked, bells announced it was time to go to a room with whitewashed walls. And when he was asked to say what he learned from homework, he thought in feelings, and didn't know how to avoid a teacher's punches to the solar plexus delivered to provoke better answers. During recesses from cramming dates in which emperors defeated kings, he didn't want to battle for turf on the playground with the children of the ones who remapped the uplands. Consequently, he walked alone beside walls topped with broken glass, and he befriended ants that lived in cracks in the cement, feeding them grains of sugar bunched in the heel of his pockets. When he returned to class, he peered out dusty windows, composing letters to the dead to remember them better.

Every night, the air creaked with the bones of old boys who'd won silver trophies that now lined glass cabinets in corridors, and he hid in the open, waiting for sleep to take Einhart Herrmann on the top bunk, Einhart Herrmann, whose father shot natives from the bed of his jeep during the uprisings encouraged by those in jail cells.

Jalousies heaved, and Woloff lay on bedsprings, measuring the value of filling goals in faraway places with soccer balls, and of buying the studs worn by the free-kick specialist from an English coal town. In subsequent months, he charted his progress on a schedule sent by Uncle Phineas, and ran hexagonals on rain-drenched grass until he was unclear whether his right thigh would easily mend from these torments. Woloff entered mile races on the track and easily won them. Then he slept in snippets, more or less, awakening more and more with the memory of his dead mama's black porridge on his tongue. As a sixteen-year-old at the IAAF World U20 Championships, he pressed much earlier than planned, reaching the bell lap of the 1,500 in world junior record pace. He relaxed, and accelerated on the back stretch, half expecting that, at any moment, the others would creep up on his shoulder as the finish line bobbled into view. He shut his eyes, and when he opened them the unofficial clock beside the track had him at 3.28.31, a new record.

Uncle Phineas had one basic rule. Woloff must never goof off. Never. Ever. Chop, chop, he said whenever Woloff slept past seven-thirty in the morning. It was an expression he had picked up from Rita Oozol, who used it in *Switcher*.

"Chop, chop." He tugged the blanket off Woloff. "*Ni wakati wa kwenda kukimbia.*"[1]

Woloff pulled the blanket back up to his chin. "I'm up."

"No, you're not." Uncle Phineas shook him by the shoulders. "Stop goofing off!" The *fundi*[2] that graduated *maxima cum laude* with a doctorate in philosophy now ran a garage as the only mechanic in the area. "To want is to be willing," he said, paraphrasing Nietzsche.

"That doesn't help," Woloff replied, tying his braids with an ochre cloth.

---

1. It's time to go run.
2. mechanic

Uncle Phineas laughed. "It's the best I can do for such a hostile audience."

On his way out the bedroom, Uncle Phineas stopped at a desk. He picked up a notebook, opened it, and looked for signs of a life he suspected his nephew had on the down low.

"*Mjomba!*"[1] Woloff said. "That's private."

"What's this you're writing?" Uncle Phineas asked, pointing to the page.

"It's not mine," Woloff replied. "That's all Precious."

He coughed into a handkerchief. "*Kwa nini una hiyo?*"[2]

"She wants to know if it's a good story."

"I didn't know she's a writer."

"Don't sound so surprised," Woloff replied.

"I always see her goofing off." He placed the notebook back on the desk. "*Kama wewe.*"[3]

Woloff stood up. "I'm going," he said.

"Stay off the main road," Uncle Phineas replied. "Convoys of mercenaries have been seen passing by."

Soon Woloff ran along the unpaved road leading to a red-brick chapel and passed Mary and Sarah Kapalei, who wore cotton dresses that covered their knees. Next to them strode Peter Koinet and Paul Naisianoi, the Christian converts who accompanied them wearing charcoal trousers, black ties, and white short-sleeved shirts. They all carried black leather Bibles that went with them everywhere, even to the toilet.

"*Mungu akubariki,*"[4] they said.

"Live long and prosper," Woloff replied.

The foursome returned to chat about a scripture that

---

1. Uncle
2. Why do you have that?
3. Like you.
4. God bless.

spoke to them of how to keep their future, theoretical marriages sound, and Woloff moved on between the stalks of sugar cane at Mr. Leboo's multi-acre farm. Then he pushed open a wooden gate and ran down a path discernible only by tire tracks in ankle-deep grass. At a yellow plain among purple catacombs, Woloff looked at his wristwatch and concentrated on briskly moving his feet. He breathed deeply while passing the last of a series of red anthills, threw in a surge next to patches of spiked thorn bushes in an everglade of orange flowers, and turned right at the village.

He stopped and checked his time. He'd closed in 4:17 over the final mile. Wiping sweat off his forehead with his T-shirt, he walked past Leboo's convenience store, which also served as a bank, a post office, a public telephone, and an internet service. West along the dusty main road, he stopped to greet an aged Namunyak, who sat on a stool in front of her hut.

"*Kijana*,[1] did you hear about Shadrack Mejooli?" she asked him.

"No, Namunyuk." Shadrack had a reputation as a collaborator with mercenaries who'd been raiding farms in the area.

"He is with the unDead," she said.

Woloff was silent.

"It was two days after he threw away the boma root I put on his father's grave for protection," she said. "He told all the people gathered that Namunyuk is superstition." She beckoned Woloff to stand closer to her. "As the knowledge holders say, when a big man travels far from the settlement, he forgets the way back to the morning star."

"Yes, Namunyuk."

"*Alikuwa na kiburi*."[2] She reached into a bag for her gourd

1. Young man
2. He was arrogant.

and shook the pebbles that lived in it. "Are you also a big man, Woloff?"

"No," he replied. "That would be Shadrack."

She laughed, holding the gourd to an ear before she spilled its contents onto the dust at her feet.

Woloff was usually skeptical about...well, just about everything. However, Namunyuk communed with black suns that devoured time. She sliced cuts of meat from the hind legs of goats, smeared them onto the bellies of those who were ill, and believers sat up the next morning ready to gallop through the surrounding plains without traces of the un-Dead's stink on them.

"You will be going to America soon," she said.

"Tomorrow." Woloff pointed at the scattered pebbles. "Unless they are telling you something different."

"*Hakuna kitu,*"[1] she replied.

"What's nothing?"

"Nothing is nothing," she replied.

"*Asante,*[2] Namunyuk," he said, thinking how unhelpful she was being.

* * *

In the time Woloff knew Precious, she'd only asked one thing of him—to formally meet her mother before he left the continent. Therefore, on his final evening in the country, Mama Precious greeted him in her doorway. He wore an overlarge suit as they stood among rusty shacks and preternaturally rib-caged dogs.

---

1. There's nothing.
2. Thank you

"Welcome," she said. She was tall and had high cheekbones like her daughter, wore a yellow dress with a matching wrap around her head, and carried a baby in her arms.

Woloff followed her into a room with four fruit crates, a kerosene lamp, and a transistor radio tuned to a cricket match on the BBC.

"*Kaa chini*,"[1] she said.

He got comfy on a crate while two more children ran through the door in khaki shorts. He fiddled with a clip on his tie and answered questions while Precious waited for him outside.

"Who is your family?" Mama Precious asked.

"My father is Nampazo, and my mother is Abdalla, ma'am," he said. "My ancestors left Lake Turkana when Engai Narok warned of the great famine, and they settled on the shores of Lake Victoria."

"And both your father and mother have passed?"

"Yes," he replied. "I live with my uncle the fundi."

"May peace be with them," she said.

Woloff stared at cracks in the dung floor.

"Do not forget that a zebra takes its stripes wherever it goes," she continued.

"Yes, Mama Precious," he replied.

"What then is in your *baadaye*?"[2] she asked.

"I'm going on a scholarship to run in America," he said.

"*Kukimbia*?"[3] she asked.

"*Ndiyo*,"[4] he replied.

---

1. Sit down.
2. future
3. To run?
4. Yes.

She put the baby against her chest and rubbed his back. "Are you faster than Filbert Bayi?"

He laughed. "I am now, after doing hills like him," he said. "I plan to win the 1,500 at the Olympics next year by running at the front like he used to."

"I like your *kujiamini*,"[1] she said. "The village which is not discussed is not built."

"When I graduate, I'll return home to marry your daughter." Woloff was sweating at the collar. "Afterwards, I'd like to build and run a training camp for young athletes here."

Mama Precious told one of the children to fetch Precious, and then gently rocked the baby in her arms while they waited in silence.

Precious came in wearing a white dress with frilly hems and nervously played with a string that dangled from a sleeve.

"Did he tell any of his jokes?" she asked.

"Do you have a joke to tell me, Woloff?" Mama Precious said.

"Unfortunately, no," he replied. "I can't remember any of the ones I hear. So I'm going to spare you having to listen to me get one wrong."

Mama Precious got serious. "You must encourage each other," she said. "We only have this one life, and it is important that you encourage one another as you make your way in it. One finger does not kill a louse."

"*Asante*,[2] Mama," Precious said.

"I'll remember that," Woloff added.

"How will you remember, Woloff?" Mama Precious said. "Did you not say you cannot remember jokes?"

1. confidence
2. Thank you

* * *

Woloff and Precious hid under moonlight in a hollowed-out patch in Mr. Ramala's sugar-cane field. It was dead quiet, and they sat back-to-back smoking weed. Yes, they passed it back and forth like a couple of fancy lovers in one of those Godard films they watched in a cinema in town.

"Bless up, Woloff," Precious said.

They closed their eyes and didn't count on the certainty of the days ahead.

Precious belonged to a world made up of those who'd die with their comrades for the ideologies they believed in. At war, they fought for a new constitution, chewed khat, slept in the Magogo Forest with rifles, went out on foot patrols in minefields, got in deadly firefights, and captured prisoners. Woloff didn't know specifics. There were rumours, of course. Kidnappings. Torture. Bombings. Nothing easy to prove. On returning home for short spells, Precious would be wired, closing bars, or partying hard until dawn in the forest. She didn't go to church or follow the teachings of Namunyuk. Instead, she read Franz Fanon and wrote or, at least, she scribbled down her thoughts in bits and parts. Why were they together? Precious liked to watch Woloff train and take trips with him to the city to watch foreign movies. He enjoyed the way she used grand hand gestures to explain whisking discourse, riffing about automatons and machinic systems that devoured the planet. Then they threw sex at the deepest part of the night. They threw it in front of the windows in his bedroom, curtain open. They did it standing beside the dresser. They did it for hours in sugar-cane fields.

"I'll be back to marry you," Woloff said.

"Fuck that," she replied. "You say this because leaving is

sad. But once you're far from here, you won't understand why you ever felt that way."

"Not true."

"Fuck it all," she said, handing him the last pull on the spliff.

Sure, she was into him, but they were individuals first. No question.

"Do whatever the fuck," she said.

She turned around, pulled him down to the ground with her, and manoeuvred him until his head was on her belly. Then she gently cupped the back of his neck with a hand. "And if you ever think of reasons why I might hate you, fuck that. When you go, there's no looking back. Go. Run. Win a gold medal. Set world records. Finish your degree. Get on with your life, and I'll get on with mine."

He would have objected, but he knew she was right. In the end, he'd be remembered for his accomplishments on the track and she'd live on among the martyrs who had her loyalty.

* * *

Woloff spent the rest of his night out with Precious, and as the roosters began to crow, climbed into his bedroom window and dropped past the curtain onto the floor. Uncle Phineas dozed, curled in a ball on the end of his bed.

Woloff shook him a couple of times. "I'm home," he said.

"It's after four in the morning," Uncle Phineas said.

"We lost track of the time," Woloff replied.

Anger tamped down modulations of Uncle Phineas's voice. "You need to remember that being black is like raising young ones, eh." He flicked on a lamp and searched Woloff's face for clues to help him understand his nephew. "When you have a child, you have to feed it, correct? Even if you hate work, you have to do it to make money."

"I don't follow," Woloff said, puzzled.

"Being black is like that," he replies. "It comes with responsibilities."

Woloff nodded.

"Take Aristotle." The fundi had been rereading passages of *Nicomachean Ethics* while he waited for customers to show up in their muddy vehicles. "Be the best you can be. The four cardinal virtues. Wisdom. Moderation. Courage. Justice." He held up four fingers. "And the greatest of these is what? Moderation. And this is what? Balance. Now, if we return to my original point. Being black is understanding that one's only option is to be the best one can be through balanced judgment."

"Like a parent?"

"*Ndiyo!*"[1]

"You can't lead on the track if you don't handle your responsibilities off it," he said. "You're fit. You'll win that gold medal at the Olympics if you push the pace. Don't lose focus."

"I had a long night." Woloff limped toward his closet. "Can this wait until I've had sleep?"

"Are you hurt?" Uncle Phineas asked.

"I twisted my knee a little," he replied. "It'll be fine."

"Let me look at it," Uncle Phineas said.

"I'm good," Woloff replied. "Truly."

Once he was alone in his bedroom, Woloff curled under covers among thoughts of the witch doctor, Namunyuk, and

---

1. Yes!

her inability to see his future in the pebbles. Did she see nothing, or was there just no future for him? His knee hurt and he thought of Precious, the tomboy whose project was to carry out her own self-destruction. They'd spent most of the night hiding from mercenaries in the Magogo Forest, and Woloff clearly saw the limits of his own willingness to enter Precious's violent world. What the hell was he thinking? He was going to be an Olympic champion.

* * *

Nothing works as planned. On Woloff's trip to the airport, insurgents seized the main broadcasting company television station. Flights were cancelled, the airport closed, and, in the late evening, he found himself herded with other passengers into the Hilton in the capital's centre. There wasn't any electricity, the phone and internet services were cut, and he was stuck in his hotel room without a clue as to what was happening. Behind drawn curtains, he sat on his bed twisting his braids, trying to summon up the courage to join the other stranded travellers gathered at the bar.

There was a knock at the door.

"Who is it?" he asked.

"Lemasolai Mayasi," a lawyer he met on the bus responded. "I'm in the room across the hall."

Woloff opened the door. "What's up?"

"It's best to stay in your room until the morning," said Lemasolai.

"Okay," Woloff replied.

"Keep away from your windows," Lemasolai continued. "You don't want to give snipers anything to shoot at." He looked at a wristwatch. "And please, don't under any circumstances let anyone into your room. Looters are a real danger."

"Got it."

"Take courage," Lemasolai said. "And remember that our Lord and Saviour has a plan. One day, his reasons for all this will be made known to us."

"*Asante*, Lemasolai!"

Woloff shut the door, barricaded himself in with a dresser, and pulled his mattress to the floor. Then he laid out of sight of sharpshooters. It was pitch-black, so he couldn't do much except wait. The back of his knee ached. The night keeled with random gunfire, wailing. A bomb exploded. The hotel's foundations shook. His walls creaked, and he checked his cellphone again for service. He'd been trying to reach Uncle Phineas to let him know he was safe, but he couldn't get a signal. He crawled away into a corner before curling into a ball, flinching with each burst of automatic gunfire. Sometimes it was close enough that his windowpanes shook, at other times it was a long ways off in another part of the city. There was no pattern to it, and his fate seemed random. A throw of the pebbles. A chance encounter. He remembered Namunyak and wondered if this was what she meant when she told him she saw nothing in his prediction. What is nothing? Death? Not existing? Another blast nearby set off car alarms. He imagined convoys of soldiers pulling up in armoured vehicles and jeeps, storming into the hotel, and shooting everyone. Him. Time slurred, and it was a shock to his system when darkness finally gave way to a smattering of grey.

* * *

Knuckles banged on his door. "Good morning!" Lemasolai said.

"One second." Woloff groggily stumbled over to the barricades and pulled aside the dresser before opening the door.

Lemasolai got to the point. "The hotel is on the outskirts of government-held territory," he said. "And the insurgents are pushing inward." Lemasolai handed him two cans of passion-fruit juice. "Be smart and stay in your room as much as possible."

For the rest of the morning, Woloff didn't know what narrative would choose him. He reinforced his barricades by pushing his bed frame against the dresser. Then he rubbed a tender bump behind his knee, wishing he'd asked Lemasolai for food.

Lying in this room, waiting for death, he was angry with himself for not being better prepared for the unexpected.

* * *

Late afternoon, Lemasolai knocked again.

Woloff hurled aside the barricade and let him in. "Tell me you've got good news!" he said.

"The government's back in control of the capital," Lemasolai said. "Troops will be coming tomorrow to escort international visa holders to the airport."

Woloff hugged him.

* * *

At a checkpoint on the road to the airport, Woloff sat at the back of a bus, clutching his passport, while two government soldiers in baggy greens walked in. Strapped with rifles, they marched to a seat at the back.

"*Pasipoti?*"[1]

A man in a charcoal suit fumbled in a bag and then peered up at them, holding a handful of cash.

Briskly, they wrestled the man out of his seat, bills fluttering around them as they shoved him along the aisle.

"Help me!" he pleaded.

No one budged.

"Please help me!"

The man was shoved out the doors and onto the sidewalk.

As the bus pulled away, he was surrounded by soldiers pointing rifles at him.

Woloff's mind reeled multifariously.

* * *

Upon his arrival on the island, Woloff struggled to make impressions in his head again. People standing outside baggage check were animated shapes and moving shades of meanings that left him puzzled. Inanimate signs told him where to go, but he couldn't get his feet to take him there. Sadness ached in his joints, and as he sat in a cab on his way through Ogweyo's Cove on the drive to campus, he fought tiredness by naming objects. There were palm trees, and yes, the majority of the trip was either on a three-lane highway packed with cars of different makes, or else through a city jam-packed with dull cement. A bank. Bus stops. What did it add up to? He repeated himself, forgot what he was trying remember, and waited for a clue that would bring him back to himself.

---

1. Passport?

Quicker than anticipated, he was deposited by cab in front of an office that was locked, and sat in a tie and jacket on the stairs while waiting outside Flanagan Hall. Thumb-sized cockroaches swarmed around his feet as he sweated what felt like blood.

A woman walked past, listening to Madonna shout from headphones over the ears of her hijab.

She stopped. "You okay?"

He pointed to the phones. "'Like a Prayer'?" he asked.

"No, 'Like a Virgin,'" she replied. "It's one my kids' CDs."

A breeze kicked up discarded paper and dust in the parking lot, and he strove to be linear in response. "I don't think you should let them listen to that."

"You think Biggie would be better."

He remembered "Ten Crack Commandments." "I misspoke. Madonna's fine."

Afrah was from China, and she was either going to or coming from her third *salah* of the day.

"That looks hot." She pointed at his suit.

"So does that," he said of her hijab, trying to seem normal.

"Here." She reached over to loosen his tie, and unbuttoned the top of his shirt. "You're buttoned up like a colonial officer."

"Colonial officer?"

"I could let you into the cafeteria until someone shows up at the front desk, if that helps. It's against policy, but it's much cooler in there."

Woloff nodded his head toward her hijab. "Isn't that breaking one of the pillars of Islam? Thou shalt not let a stranger into the cafeteria without the permission of management."

"It depends if we're talking Sharia law or not." She picked

up one of his bags and carted it off in the direction of a glass door.

Afrah saw him safely inside. Then she lurched into more of the Sharia-like laws that governed the dormitory. There was a table with three computers in front of a door leading into the kitchen. The computers were temperamental, so he wasn't supposed to bank on using them for anything other than email. The kitchen looked more like a boiler room, and she pointed to a shelf of plastic containers with names scribbled onto them in indelible ink.

"We can make our own meals," she said. "But if you do, put all foods in plastic containers to keep the cockroaches out."

There were other important items. No guests were allowed in the rooms after ten at night. No food in the rooms. No men on the second or fourth floor. No lighting up barbecues indoors. No stealing shit. And by the time the tour of the cafeteria was complete, she took him to the now-open front desk to collect the key to his dorm room.

Woloff's lodging on the third floor was a walk-in closet with a single bed, a desk, a metal chair, a lamp, and a plug-in fan. It was stark, but he had a balcony on which he could pull out his chair in order to watch scooters, rusty bicycles, and oldsters with wide-brimmed hats squat on stools while chatting with their age mates.

Gutted by his journey, he lay on the bed, worried that his body wouldn't be able to learn new habits, and that his mind would no longer be able to make sense from nonsense.

11 Days to Wedding

<u>12:02 p.m.</u> Long after Mutti has gone to work, Schuld takes the yellow meds to make the voice work that tells her to be like boys and girls who fuck each other. Then she joins P.J. in the backyard where he has a barbecue going. Her shoulder smarts and her body is sore, but she's delighted by the progress she has made on the exhibit. The bathtub is done, and she's got plans to find a discarded TV monitor to gut for parts.

On the patio, her dad-to-be bends over smoke that rises in a rotating circle from slabs of cow thighs that roast on an iron grate. He has a poker in his hand, and behind him water sprinklers blather into grass.

"Hey, buddy," P.J. says. "How's your wrist? I see you aren't wearing a bandage."

"It'll probably heal faster if I keep it mobile," she replies.

"Or make it worse."

Schuld flexes her injured wrist. "Sorry to hear about your dad."

"Thanks," he says. "He gets discharged from the hospital tomorrow. He'll be fine...if he slows down."

"What are the chances of that?" she asks.

P.J. blows onto charcoal embers. "Are you going to be home for the comet tonight? Woloff's welcome to join."

"Nah," she replies. "We're gonna watch the whole thing with real astronomers' telescopes from a rooftop. Woloff knows an astrophysicist who's hooked up."

"That's too damn lucky." P.J. jabs at the sizzling sirloins before he turns them over. "I hear you used to play soccer in high school."

"Not so much," Schuld replies, absentmindedly untangling curls in her hair.

"I played centre midfield in college." He wipes his hands on an apron with *Mum* written on it. "We won the NCAA when I was a sophomore."

"Cool."

"You were a goalkeeper, weren't you?" P.J. asks.

"Yup," Schuld replies.

"Good God, a goalie," he says. "Our best one graduated after we were national champs, and the whole team went pear-shaped after that. For the rest of my career, we had to make do with a guy who was a freakin' sieve."

P.J. brushes barbecue sauce onto meat and talks about two more related items. The right back in college had "two left feet," and the coach was "a Type-A personality, an anal-retentive control freak." Starting in her body, and stuck in her head, Schuld nods like she's supposed to until P.J. finally uses his smart phone to send pics of cooked cow parts to his Facebook friends.

"I'm gonna go skateboarding for a bit," Schuld says.

"Of course," P.J. replies. "It's your day off. Don't let me keep you."

"*Bis später,*"[1] Schuld says.

She walks to the shed at the back of the backyard, closes the door behind her, and digs out the paint thinner from behind a pile of grease-stained rags. After she listens to make sure P.J. is still on the patio, Schuld unscrews the cap and presses her nostrils to the lid. She inhales deeply, and it feels yummy from her nose to the back of her skull, where the tension lives. Then her thinking voice gets back to work in ways that make it unclear if eating cow parts is different than eating human ones.

Strapped to an iPod, Schuld hops onto her skateboard and wheels down the sidewalk into future transactions. As she rides the crest of the hot afternoon, muggy air tastes of salt. She rolls left, her headphones chirruping house beats that go bump-deep in her bone marrow. She knows Mutti is trying to make a family with P.J. based on a foundation of telling the truth, but it's an impossible situation. It seems... unrealistic. Utopian. Take the semi-automatic handgun she got on the darknet—would she ever tell Mutti about it? No way. Forget it. In principle, Schuld ought to be open with her mother about the things she needs to know, but if she mentions the weapon, Mutti will flip. Dipping right, she skates over rutted, rattled cement. Her auburn mane jostles. Sadness lifts a little, and then retreats into a rift where goats used to live behind a fence that runs long with glinting iron. She waits for a convoy of Humvees to pass on their way to Huntington Barracks; soldiers smudged with camouflage paint sweat in desert gear behind mounted machine guns. Then she hops a curb, crosses onto a bicycle path, and coasts along beside lots filled with men in con-

---

1. See you later.

struction boots who wander through skeletons of unfinished buildings.

It feels fabulous to not be harassed for a moment about the correct way to have thoughts. So she stops at the bridge to watch white egrets sit in trees lining a stream. Carefully folding and putting away tension, she chews on cotton balls soaked in crushed Ramazipan. Soon she's off-key, deliciously unable to keep level. She thinks of the stories she tells Mutti about herself and of how the telling always changes. Why? Because if she wants her mother to understand whatever it is she wants her to understand, Schuld needs to focus more on certain parts of what she tells than others. There's no way she's saying anything to Mutti about the gun. No flipping way. She fucking well doesn't want or need to be told what to do.

Schuld screeches, and a congregation of egrets flutters from tree branches. Then she moves again, skating toward Kutama Point, a neighbourhood with rows of cement houses bunched together beside the Alto Pyramid, where the majority of its residents work.

Schuld glides beside a field overgrown with weeds and turns when she reaches a side street weighed down by electric wires that sag from poles. After a quick right at a pile of black garbage bags ripped open by dogs, she picks up her board and walks beside election signs mixed in among clotheslines hung with bright-red-and-orange prints. Little boys and girls romp behind chain-link fences among tires scattered in wild tufts of grass, or climb into the back of pickup trucks parked in yards next to orange pylons lifted from construction sites. Nearby, adults huddle together in shade on front steps, or tinker around in driveways under the hoods of cars near piles of crumbling bricks.

Once Schuld reaches the middle of the street, she turns where a shopping cart rusts upside down on a patch of dirt and knocks on the door of a pea-green house, anxiety tagging her while tension mixes with a buildup of wax on follicles in her ears. Woloff opens up. His gangly frame hangs on to bones that jut beneath his T-shirt at shoulders and his shorts at hips.

"Want some company at your doctor's appointment?"

"Sure," he says. "Come in a sec while I get my gear."

Schuld steps over a gaggle of running shoes in the entrance and follows him into a living room that reeks of pot. His roommate, Bill Tilson, a shot putter on the OCU track team, lies on a couch with a gas-mask bong on his face watching local celebrity Rita Oozol in an infomercial to promote a new line of her handcrafted fork rings. Schuld goes with Woloff to his bedroom, and she waits while he clears a weighing scale and zip-lock bags from his mattress. Then he dumps them on the bottom shelf of a closet full of mason jars, bags with buds of weed, and several motorbike helmets. Woloff closes the door behind him before he padlocks it shut.

"Here." He throws Schuld a couple of dime bags. "I just re-upped on sativa, so if you need more, just ask."

"Cool," Schuld replies, stuffing them into a pocket in her shorts.

Woloff dips a ball of cotton in face powder, looks in the closet mirror, and makes a mustard circle around his right eye. Then he slips bronze bangles onto his arms. "Ready," he says.

In the living room, Bill pulls off his bong mask and sits up. "You taking off?"

"Yup," Woloff replies. "I'm going to see the doctor about my knee."

"Can you pick up some chips and a bottle of orange soda on your way home?" Bill asks.

"Done," Woloff replies.

Bill refocuses on lighting up.

As they leave, Schuld notices a picture of Woloff's dad in combat gear on the wall. He stands with a rifle looped over his shoulder and his pants tucked into his boots.

"Your dad looks young in that picture," she says.

"He was twenty-five," he replies. "It's the last one of him alive."

"You look a lot like him."

"That's what Uncle Phineas says."

Out on the street, the neighbours' pit bull barks at them from the end of a chain attached to a pole. Woloff limps as they walk past Governor Gary Ostheim's territory, his blue-and-white posters driven with stakes into the ground.

"Your grandfather is popular," Woloff says.

"Correct."

"Can I meet him?" Woloff asks.

"A transgender granddaughter and her boyfriend isn't a good look for the campaign," she replies. "He's hasn't adapted well to my changes, so we don't talk anymore."

"Jesus!" Woloff says.

They walk past plastic swimming pools and turn at the end of the block onto a dirt path that cuts through a field overgrown with weeds. Overhead, a helicopter equipped with a camera crew carries VIPs, strapped in at window seats, to take pics of the famous tail of water that plummets a full kilometre at M'Toma Falls.

"I'm not a fan of our governor." Schuld flexes her injured wrist. "He's a pragmatist who's into banks and privatizing prisons. He's the opposite of everything I believe in."

"What's with your hand?" Woloff asks.

Schuld tells him about the transphobes who attacked her, and about her injuries. She's rattled, but fine, mostly. "I'm okay," she says. "I'm just having a hard time adjusting to being outside at night again."

"Motherfuckers," Woloff replies, wondering why she didn't tell him earlier.

"I'm not going to the cops," Schuld says. "That's what Mutti would suggest if I told her about it, but making out a report while I get gawked at like some sort of freak isn't helpful."

He's afraid for her. "I'm picking you up from the studio tonight," he says.

"Much appreciated." Tears prick in her eyes. "I feel sick thinking about it."

"This has to stop."

"I don't know how to make that happen."

Flummoxed, they push back weeds that bend across the path, round a corner, and enter a field of desiccated macadamia nut shrubs. Silently, they walk through row after row of shrivelled bushes, a red light on a small drone darting around in the sky above them.

3:39 p.m. After an ultrasound on his knee shows abnormal thickening around his iliotibial band, Woloff gets a cortisone injection and a recommendation to get arthroscopic surgery as soon as possible. Within the hour a searing pain flares up in the back of his leg, a migraine settles in his temples, and he's staggered by hot flashes. Now he limps toward his under-the-table job at the home of the Sunderlands, a rapidly constructed house with the facade of a country estate. He hobbles past a front garden with sprinklers that go on regularly at four in the morning and makes his way along a pathway that leads up past a campaign yard sign for Governor Ostheim to a brass knocker the shape of a gargoyle.

* * *

4:13 p.m. "You're thirteen minutes late," Eve Sunderland says, staring at the mustard circle thickly powdered around his eye. "I was about to send out for a search party."

"Sorry about that, Mrs. Sunderland," he says. "I left a message about an appointment to see a doctor."

"It's fine," she replies, her voice tight with irritation.

The front hall is free of clutter. A vacuumed beige carpet is spread beneath stills of mallard ducks and green apples in brown bowls. Through a door frame is a kitchen with glinty, sterile surfaces, and a sparkling coffee maker with what appears to be a GPS tracking system affixed to its shiny face. All of the wiped surfaces lend the place a tasteful gentility. Mrs. Sunderland stands on the bottom of her carpeted staircase, calling upward for Rick. Then she excuses herself before disappearing into the living room to continue a meeting.

As Woloff stoops to remove his shoes, a thump of feet erupts at the top of a staircase, and before he can get his balance, the Sunderlands' sixteen-year-old son barrels down to give him a hug.

"Steady there, soldier." Woloff gently disentangles himself from the boy's embrace.

Rick turns and rushes into his dad's study at the end of the hallway with Woloff in pursuit. He plunks himself down in a chair, then rocks back and forth, banging his back hard against its leather backing.

Woloff places a hand firmly behind Rick's head. "Are you

up for a trip to the beach? We haven't done that in a while."

Rick leaps up, hop-steps out the door, and disappears into women's voices in the living room.

"Shit!" Woloff says.

He's careful not to push his leg as he follows Rick and finds him standing in front of a coffee table arranged for late-afternoon tea. Still as a statue, he stares at a group of three huddled on the couch, his arms folded around his upper body.

Mrs. Sunderland has been calmly addressing Mrs. Sienna Moorland and Mrs. Paige Cargan, two volunteers from Ronson Street Baptist Church. "You've certainly come a long way since you moved back here from that poorly run facility, dear," she says to her son.

"Rick!" Woloff whispers. "We're interrupting."

"The latest medication hasn't helped get your sleep under control, has it, angel?" Mrs. Sunderland says. "But at least you don't have as many seizures."

Woloff clasps firmly on to his arm. "Come on, soldier."

"Dr. Salsman thinks you belong at Waybridge Care." Mrs. Sunderland's modulated voice exerts its dominion over the scene. "But you belong at home, don't you, dear?"

Rick doesn't budge but continues to watch the women from church without blinking.

"I don't remember who said it first," Mrs. Moorland interjects. "But one never knows who one's teacher is." She stands, extending a hand. "You are my teacher, Rick."

Her teacher's shin bumps against the coffee table, and teacups wobble before righting themselves.

Mrs. Sunderland dabs a serviette into small puddles of spilled tea. "You're doing much, much better at home, aren't you, my dear?" she says.

"We should leave," Woloff says.

"Yes, it's time to go, honey," Mrs. Sunderland says. "But don't forget to stay away from the water. You get far too excited and I don't want you wading in and getting your clothes wet."

This time Woloff is forceful in gripping Mrs. Moorland's teacher firmly by a forearm before he directs him out of the room. Once in the hallway, he points to a closet full of footwear. "We've gotta get."

Rick grumbles while he helps himself to scuffed running shoes, sits on a bottom stair, slips them on, and ties up his laces. Then Woloff points to the front door and waits for him to twist open a lock.

Once outdoors, Rick runs into the driveway to the family station wagon and pulls repeatedly on the door handle.

"Be patient, dude." Woloff unlocks the door and steps back while Rick gets comfortable in the passenger seat. "You're going to have to do up your seat belt."

Rick giggles and fiddles with dials on the radio.

"Nah, soldier. Your belt?" Rick ignores him, and Woloff has to work to hold Rick's hand to the seat belt as he gets him to do it up on his own. By the time Woloff is settled next to him, Rick rocks back and forth in his seat.

The car turns left and then loops right as they ride the long tarmac spine of a road that runs up a gradual summit adjacent to the ocean. Rick's window is open just enough for him to lean into a breeze that tickles the brim of his red beach cap. Gauzy sky meets a distant horizon punctured by cruise ships. Closer still, frothy waves carry surfers, as well as windsurfers with sails that flap while they await the next wave that turns from turquoise to dull green. Rick's rocking quickens as the car enters the first of many homes in

Granger's Grove. It's challenger Colin Riverdale's turf, and his posters line the front of hedges of purple bougainvilleas and roiling pink flowers. Locals for hire take weed whackers to the overgrowth at the borderlines of driveways, and inhabitants get in and out of washed cars among fountains with statues of boyish cherubim that spit water from their dicks. The station wagon passes under monkey pods into shade, spotty pearls of sun peeking through cracks in the foliage. At a stop sign, they wait as a dog walker takes a pack of six through the intersection in a breeze that kicks with moisture and softens the firmament with the tinge of blue delphiniums.

"We're here," Woloff says, turning into a parking lot along the edge of a sandy cliff that overlooks the beach, the radio buzzing jingles as they idle into a vacant spot.

Rick is quick to undo his seat belt, and after Woloff opens his door, he charges outside. They follow a black rail that leads to where the trail sharply descends between tall, yellow grass. Then Woloff takes Rick by the hand and they walk down the slope that leads through ginger bushes opening onto Ka'alipo Beach. Rick breaks free and rushes forward to stand near a bubbling, dying wave. Then he jumps away before he examines his footprints left in the wet sand.

"Yo, soldier!" Woloff stands behind him. "Your mom will kill me if you get your shoes wet."

Startled by a spearfisher in black wetsuit emerging from deeper water, Rick's off again, chasing a scrum of cawing gulls.

"Jesus, Rick." Woloff goes after him as he rounds a bluff claimed by green umbrellas and even greener lounge chairs. Then he watches in alarm as Rick stumbles among women face down with strapless, oily backs, and men who wear thongs with their shiny butt cheeks thrust into the dying sunlight.

"Stop!" Woloff shouts.

Rick knocks over a Styrofoam cooler, spilling ice and beer cans, while he approaches a group of children who toss sand with red plastic shovels beside a sign that warns of an infestation of jellyfish. Woloff limp-runs as Rick hop-skips toward the deserted beach before jumping into waves.

About ten metres into shallow rocky water, Rick stumbles and falls down. Then he thrashes around, screaming. Woloff splashes toward him, grips him by the arm, and tries to lift him to his feet. Rick struggles out of his grasp. "Rick!" Woloff lunges forward and tackles him. They both topple into the water. Woloff's knee slams against a rock. He grabs on to his leg, a surge of pain coursing through him. As he gains his bearings, he sees Rick leap up before swiping at a jellyfish on his back. Behind him in the water, the head of a dead foal is caught between tentacles of coral in a reef.

* * *

5:21 p.m. Woloff adds it up. He re-injured his knee. Rick has welts from three jellyfish stings on his back and shoulders. They found a dead foal. Now he sits across from the Sunderland's at their kitchen table.

"What were you doing by the water?" Mr. Sutherland asks, his skin red with fury.

"He bolted away unexpectedly," Woloff says, playing with the bangles on his arm.

"I distinctly told you to stay away from the water," Mrs. Sutherland replies. "This isn't the sort of thing Rick can unsee. My Lord! He'll take a long time to recover physically and mentally from this."

"A long, long time," Mr. Sunderland adds.

"We've been overlooking things," she says.

"The makeup," Mr. Sunderland says.

"Yes, the makeup," she says. "You don't seem to be showing much good sense these days."

"Or the least bit of common sense."

"And we can't afford to put Rick at that kind of risk."

The circumstance is too extreme to overlook. Police were involved. Rick needed to be sedated, and the dosage of his medication adjusted. There are questions Woloff can't answer about being near a beach with a jellyfish warning, so the Sunderlands fire him without praying about it first.

Three hours later, he's at a party thrown by George Chang, a 10,000-metre runner who studies astrophysics. Dispirited, he sits on a paisley couch beneath a replica of the universe projected onto the living room ceiling, stewing about Schuld. She shooed him away from sHipley's when he went to pick her up earlier because of the opening tomorrow night. She still had more to do, and said she'd get a ride from Demarion. Fine. But the comet's happening soon, and she hasn't shown up yet. Could she be hurt? Or worse? He checks his messages again and leaves her another one, angry that she's making him worry about her.

To calm himself, Woloff rolls a spliff that he shares with Carlos Sanchez, the 800-metre runner whose father drives refrigerated trucks hauling meat. They're joined by Bill Tilson, who works as a guard at a prison during the summer (same as his father does all year round), and Jim Wilts, the steeplechaser who delivers bottled water from a warehouse to supermarkets during the off-season. Fly MC's rap on a CD player—Michie Mee, Foxy Brown, Ol' Dirty Bastard, Snoop Dogg—and no one talks about anything Woloff knows much about. There are lakes at which to get hammered on long summer weekends and motorboats and bowling leagues and skating rinks. They gossip about how Tiffany Karlsonn, the 400 hurdler, is pregnant with high jumper Ulrich Fenstermacher's child. Then, without warning, Carlos Sanchez gets up to go play chicken on the street with oncoming traffic while Bill Tilson and Jim Wilts get in an argument over the wisdom of certain fantasy football picks.

Woloff gets a text from Schuld.

Working won't make it. Gonna stay at the gallery tonight. ☹

"Holla," George interrupts.

"Yo!" Woloff replies.

"There's a helluva lot more people here than the plan," George says. "We were invaded by a bunch of botanists, and so it might be a mad scramble to get to a telescope on the roof." Then he's off to entertain a group of astronomers who crack one another up by describing what element on the periodic table they are most like.

"Come on, Fred. Manganese? Try cadmium," one says.

"Cadmium? Have you lost your effing mind?" the other replies.

"Typical cadmium response."

"Sounds more manganese to me."

There's yelling in the vicinity of the astronomers. "Two minutes till the comet!"

Woloff joins a stampede of astrophysicists who crowd the

stairs on their way to the telescopes on the roof. He nudges past Manganese. Then Cadmium. The back of his right leg twinges again, and by the time he's collected himself and made it through to the landing upstairs, all the telescopes are taken.

Miffed, Woloff stares up at the sky, looking at a shitty naked-eye's view of the comet that won't visit earth's atmosphere for another thousand years.

Words don't fit.

11 Days to Wedding

<u>7:05 p.m.</u> P.J. looks forward to the positive change in his fortunes he envisions the comet will bring along with its gases and dust that formed the sun. All told, he has picked a pack of pickled peppers and it's difficult to know how many pickled peppers in a pack of peppers he has picked. He's got to be out of his apartment before the wedding and there's packing to do. However, he's distracted as he pulls handfuls of softbacks from shelves and places them into a box. Money's tight, and they're still spending it fist over heel. The caterer needs to be paid half his fee in advance and since P.J. won't get the damage deposit until after the honeymoon, he has no quick way to raise cash. Packing boxes and tape cost him a bundle, so he needs another three hundred bucks for movers. He needs to talk to Pop about the beach house. If he can get a break from paying rent the first year, he and Kerstin can focus on paying debts and saving money. The old man's been released from hospital and confined to bed rest. Therefore, any talk with him will have to wait a couple more days.

Kerstin peeps out from behind a stack of boxes. "Did you know I have a very long tongue?"

"When you say long, do you mean like okapi long?"

"Anteater."

"Have you measured it?" P.J. stops packing. "And what did you use, a tape or a ruler?"

"I've never measured it," she replies. "However, I can clean my eyebrows with it."

"What about catching flies?"

"Oh, shit!" she says. "It's time."

"For the comet?" he asks.

"*Nein, mein Schatz.*[1] For the cream."

"Already?"

"I'm supposed to put it on every six hours."

Kerstin turns around to let him reacquaint his fingers with the wispiness of her hips. Then he performs a necessary expedition, with his thumb pressing cream onto aching muscles on her lower back.

"My girlfriends with long tongues have complained that they want sex more than their boyfriends. In fact, the other day we talked about how much we love our long tongues, and sex, and in our ideal world we would fuck at least once a day. All kinds of it too, fast and hard and slow with a sweaty, happy break in between."

He steps back for the long view. "I'm going to have to lower the waistband of the panties," he says.

"My panties!" she replies.

"As a precautionary measure," he says.

"Precautionary, huh?" Her voice has dropped an octave, and he doesn't quite know what to make of her tone.

P.J. nods, sliding down the elastic waistband.

Kerstin sighs, pretty much.

---

1. No, my sweetheart.

"Sorry," he says.

"No. It's nice," she replies.

She turns and kisses him. He squirms slightly, his mind receding to a memory of his father with an IV drip in his purple-veined hand. Metal on her wristwatch cuts into his upper abdomen, and when she drags her hand to his fly, he shuts his eyes.

Afterwards they fall apart, frisson gargling in their wind-pipes.

"Wanna ditch the comet and catch a late movie?" she asks.

"God, yes," he replies.

"We can watch a video of it online," she says.

"The colour and angles will be better," he replies.

* * *

8:40 p.m. Kerstin squeezes P.J.'s hand while they take a bus bumping along a cobblestone road that descends into a dock beside a frigid, filthy river. She tells him how difficult it was with Schuld during their trip to the cemetery in the morning. "I love by worrying," she says. "And it's worse when she's evasive. I imagine the worst. I can't stop myself, and the only thing that brings me any peace is when she's at home. I hate to admit it, but I worry about her safety, always, and her late nights at the art gallery and about all the hours she spends on the computer and with Woloff. It endlessly consumes me."

While Kerstin tells him about her daughter, the back of P.J.'s neck is clammy with sweat. She belongs to a segment of the population that talks about feeling affects and the memories that trigger them, and it makes him nervous.

"Enough about Schuld," she says. "How are you doing?"

"You mean, like emotionally?" P.J. replies.

"I just... It must be difficult with how big a personality your father is." She speaks fast. "And with everything so unsettled with our living situation, his accident can't be a simple thing for you to deal with."

"I'm not upset, if that's what you're asking."

"Really?"

"He's stubborn and refused to listen to his doctor's warnings to change his lifestyle." P.J.'s not used to making connections with people by talking about feelings. "So I hope this scare gets him to slow down."

"I don't imagine it was easy being the boss's son on a plantation," she says. "It must have been confusing, especially since your mama was from the island."

He's uncomfortable.

"If you don't mind me asking," she continues, "what happened between you and your father that makes you so terrified of talking to him about the beach house? It seems like a good thing for him to get rent for a house he doesn't use."

"It's not like that," P.J. responds.

"Did he hit you?"

He's irritated. "Well, I was hit with a belt like any other kid, I suppose," he says.

"How awful," she replies.

"It wasn't like I didn't deserve it!" he says. "I could be obnoxious."

"It's appalling," she replies. "You were just a kid."

"Is it okay if we don't talk about this?" P.J. says. "Putting it into words seems...wrong somehow."

"No, no! I didn't mean to... It's just..." she says. "You didn't deserve it."

"You misunderstand," he replies. "It's really not a traumatic thing."

As they get out of the bus in front of the 9th Street cinema, pellets of rain idle above them before listlessly touching down on their heads. She squeezes his hand and believes he needs it because his mama died, and because his pop beat him. He squeezes back because he thinks she's been hurt in her marriage, and because she's had to carry the weight of raising Schuld on her own.

* * *

9:13 p.m. Trailers give away watchable parts of upcoming attractions while Kerstin reaches into buttered popcorn glancing with technicoloured light. Thirst pilfers taste buds on her tongue, car horns up on the screen trumpet in bumper-to-bumper-sticker traffic, and she thinks of abusers, and contusions on beaten skin, and leather belts stained in blood. "You never say much about your mama," she says, naming discomforts and pushing to share sentiments about them. "What was she like?"

"Can we not do this now?" P.J. replies.

She puts her hand on his. "We're getting married in eleven days," she says.

They get quiet again.

"Mama worked at an animal shelter, and so I'd spend a lot of time on weekends walking dogs with her. One day she was working with Bensonhurst, a pit-bull mix who was shedding hair and had what looked like cigarette burns along his spine. I watched her nudge open the door of a cage, inching her way inside with a muzzle and leash in hand. Bensonhurst cringed in the back, baring teeth. She spoke in a soft voice, and once close enough, she placed the back of her hand in front of his mouth and waited out his sniffing. Afterwards she stroked the top of his head before she slipped the muzzle over his mouth and coaxed him to take a walk. When we'd gone a little over a mile it started to rain, drenching us as Bensonhurst refused to budge from the middle of a crosswalk. He braked in the centre of the intersection, his front paws digging hard into tarmac. Drivers honked horns, and Mama spoke really calmly to the dog while rain pounded us. Once she convinced Bensonhurst to cross the street, we waited under the awning outside a pawnshop for the downpour to pass.

"Mama didn't talk much, but while we waited she explained to me how she connected better with animals than with humans. No matter what she did or how flawed she was, they accepted her. And she often chose to roll around on the ground with them rather than be around people. It made her sad that she couldn't connect more with people, and most importantly with Pop, a man she married over the objections of her family."

She leans back in her seat. "Does that make you sad?"

"Not an unusual amount," he replies.

"Really?"

"For reals."

Kerstin wants to know more, but she can feel her interest is unpleasant to him. It's frustrating. She lets go of his hand and buries it in the bucket of popcorn. She didn't want to be here again, uncertain if she was being a bother because of her need to communicate.

10 Days to Wedding

<u>6:30 a.m.</u> Kerstin and P.J. are dressed in whites for a tennis match at the Woodwind Country Club on court nine.

She plays to his backhand, and despite this attack on his weakness, he's polite to her.

"Nice shot, *meine Verlobte!*"[1] he says.

"*Danke,* that was an excellent serve!" she replies.

"Better return though, much too good!" he says.

She flushes from the neck up as P.J. charges down another cross-court topspin hit to his backhand.

"Well-played, Kerstin," he says.

"Thank you, *Liebling,*"[2] she replies.

She's up two to one, so they switch sides of the court.

On serving, she rushes the net. P.J. lifts a lob over her head that drops inside the back line.

"Nice one," she says.

"I got lucky," he replies.

"Not true," she says. "You read that one well."

---

1. my fiancée!
2. darling

"*Danke*, baby," he replies.

Their politeness seems brutal in its incisive detection of a fissure developing between them, each word slicing a little deeper with a precision that leaves them both bleeding out before their workdays begin.

* * *

8:17 a.m. Kerstin hands P.J. a slice of apple strudel on a plate and sits down opposite him at his kitchen table, neither one admitting to feeling anything other than okay.

"Strooodle," he says, having a taste.

"Yup."

"Sounds a lot like poodle, doesn't it?" he says.

"Uh-huh."

There's a silence she's not okay with.

"Strooodle," she says. "It really does sound like poodle."

They get quiet again.

"I love you," he says.

"I love you too," she replies.

A song about travelling through wheat country plays on the radio as she wonders if they're pretending to be compatible. Do they communicate? Does anyone? The questions are like code she can't crack.

* * *

10:57 a.m. After parking her car at Ka'alipo Beach, Kerstin walks a pebbly incline and removes her slippers before the kilometer hike on sand to a nook curved out of rock by pounding tide. She clambers into indented stone. Rolling herself a cigarette, she peers out at surfers who brave choppy waters, and stares at the women who hover on the edges of the water, their Jack Russells playing among surfers lugging waxed boards into the ocean.

She doesn't know how to fix what she feels.

Yes, she has scars on her knees, and there are some wobbly parts at her thighs she didn't have five years ago. However, she likes all these things because they're hers. She places a hand on her solar plexus, breathing deeply from her belly and regulating the rise and fall of her stomach. She thinks about P.J., and wonders if they're following the grand narrative: girl meets boy, there's attraction, they get physical, they spend all their time together and get to know each other, they don't like each other as much as they used to, but there's now a stifling relationship with all its comforts and safety mixed in with shared responsibilities.

On the beach two women trudge past in mustard wraps, their bare feet sinking in the loose sand, and Kerstin envied that their evenings would likely end in a nightclub beneath a flutter of strobe lights. Her brain matter whooshes. Everything is motion again, and she wants this chase for something better to end.

* * *

12:31 p.m. On the terrace at Caravaccios, Jacquin de los Santos, with waves in her crimped black hair, suggests they forget about the lunch menu and focus on drinks. Kerstin calls over the waitress before Jacquin orders them a bottle of Shiraz.

"When I got up this morning I couldn't open my eyes," Jacquin says. "I've had two shows this week." She's a fashion consultant with celebrity clientele. "I lay there for at least thirty minutes. Didn't move a muscle. I thought about getting up, thought a lot actually. Then I figured I'd lie there until I felt the inclination to move."

"Have you figured out how to get the gifts back to my place from the wedding reception?" Kerstin asks.

"There was nothing on TV. And by that I mean nothing. There wasn't even a decent movie on HBO. And I didn't have the energy to flip through channels. If I turned on the computer I'd end up answering work emails, so I closed my eyes and tried to get a bit more sleep."

Kerstin struggles to pay attention. "Did you figure out how to get the gifts to my place?" she asks again.

Jacquin refills her wineglass. "Should I take them to the beach house?"

"No," Kerstin says. "That's still up in the air."

"Wow!" Jacquin replies. "Isn't that cutting it close?"

"He's got it handled," she replies.

"So take 'er easy," Jacquin says.

Kerstin laughs.

The tables around them fill with people in sunglasses who order plates of food that quickly appear before them. Jacquin holds up her drink. "To your future happiness, darling."

"*Prost.*"[1]

"Which dress have you chosen?" Jacquin refers to her gift, a short list of wedding dresses for Kerstin worn by her celebrity clientele.

"I need more time to think about it," she says. "I've been slammed with everything else."

"Is Schuld still going to be the ring bearer?"

---

1. Cheers.

"After lots of griping," Kerstin replies. "She didn't think it was something for an adult to do."

And that is their visit. They order more wine. Jacquin talks about needing to break up with a property flipper she's seeing whose second son tragically died while kayaking in rapids near M'Toma Falls. Then they make transportation arrangements. Talk about snafus with the bridal party. Take callbacks about a steamer for the wedding dress in the bridal suite.

"Thanks, Jacquin," Kerstin finally says. "You're a sweetheart."

"Are you doing okay, darling?" Jacquin asks.

Kerstin bursts into tears.

"Oh, baby." Jacquin gets up and gives Kerstin a hug.

"It'll be okay."

"It wasn't with Tobias." She refers to her ex-husband, the former organic toothpaste tycoon. "He didn't communicate either."

"P.J. is nothing like him," Jacquin says. "You'll adapt to each other's rhythms. Give it time. You two have a good thing going."

"You think?" Kerstin asks.

"Yes, he adores you," Jacquin says. "Fuck Tobias."

Tobias.

Kerstin met him twenty years ago at a press junket for *Im Chor Der Engel Stehn*[1] to write an article about local talent Rita Oozol, and her breakout supporting actress–winning role at Cannes. She'd spent two days having a variety of conversations with Rita about her childhood on the island, and her transition to playing Klara, a high-society jetsetter who

---

1. "In the choir, the angels stand." From Schiller's poem "Ode to Joy."

comes to terms with the knowledge that her life is built on a thin tissue of other people's shifting opinions. As a special guest at an after-party, Emmerich Voss, director, introduced Kerstin to Tobias Vogel, a red-haired magnate.

"Pleasure to meet you," Tobias said.

"Likewise," Kerstin replied, giddy with boredom.

"You two should know each other," Emmerich said, handing her a glass of champagne before excusing himself.

"I've no idea what he meant," she said to Tobias.

"I never know what he means," he replied. "And we've been friends since elementary school."

"Childhood friends? I don't suspect you turned out anything like him?"

"Anti-capitalist. *Nein*," he said. "We're opposites."

"Opposites?"

"I'm a realist," he said. "The market doesn't care if there are losers."

"You're a monster." She was enjoying the speedy kick of the champagne. "There probably isn't a regulation you don't imagine is dipping into your pockets to fund the Nanny State."

"Yes, I accept the verdict of the markets." He wiped a mop of red hair away from his eyes. "And I do think taxes should be lower, but how does this make me a monster?"

"Let me count the ways," she replied.

"I'm not a monster!" he exclaimed.

"Whoa," she replied. "Sensitive subject?"

He blushed. "*Entschuldigung*,"[1] he said. "You are teasing me, no?"

Since she'd be heading back to Ogweyo's Cove on a noon

---

1. Apologies.

flight in the morning, she flirted with him. It was fun for her, knowing they were so different, so there was no future in it.

By the time most of the guests had found their coats and headed into taxis or their parked cars, Kerstin and Tobias had discarded their clothes in mounds dotting the floor of his hotel room, and in the morning, over breakfast in bed, Kerstin was convinced to fly to Berlin with him for a weekend of partying, Mardi Gras–style.

* * *

At forty thousand feet, Tobias held her hand as their talk in first class centred on values.

"I grew up in a house with an ethic of togetherness," he said. "Meals at the dinner table were a focal point around which we gathered. And that means all meals. Like during the school holidays, my dad would come home for lunch so that we could all be together." While he talked about the importance of tight family units, Kerstin grasped his thick fingers and liked the quick pace at which everything whirled. Whooooosh! Whooooosh!

"I had to be quiet at dinner," Kerstin said. "There would be a discussion between my parents in which they didn't pay much attention to each other, tuning each other out as they talked over each other. After a while, she stopped trying. Then he did. Finally, we all sat around poking at food in silence."

Tobias's grip tightened.

Later that evening, they were dropped off by limo at a Marriott with an indoor fountain in the lobby. They showered before joining a friend of his at the bar for a nightcap.

Jacquin de los Santos was first to speak. "Your dress is

breathtaking." She used a crimper in her wavy dark hair. "Sleeveless black gowns never get old."

"It was a gift from Tobias," Kerstin replied.

"*Brava*,"[1] Jacquin replied. "I absolutely love classic cuts. It is..." She searched for the right word. "Breathtaking! Best. Gift. Ever."

Kerstin flushed with heat. "*Danke schön!*" she said.

"Did you see Rita Oozol's fashion meltdown on the red carpet at Cannes?" Jacquin asked. "She was all over the place with those frills. She looked like an over-embellished cake."

"Didn't you dress her?" Tobias asked.

"I usually do," Jacquin said. "She wanted to go another way this year. So thankfully that fashion disaster didn't occur on my watch."

How easy it felt for Kerstin to chit-chat beneath a Matisse. Quickly, she learned Jacquin was involved in a long-distance relationship with a financial accountant whose wife died of breast cancer, and most recently joined one of millions who sleep with a full-face mask attached to a CPAP machine for acute sleep apnea. Talking was tunnelling into root causes to produce profound truths. So she invoked and provoked feeling. Mumps in childhood. A missed opportunity to follow a dream when the money was low. And at the centre of their circle, Tobias offered practical solutions to her problems experienced in a variety of urban centres north of the Tropic of Cancer.

Kerstin felt positively Fauvist. Swept up in this merry band of winners, it became clear to her that Tobias wasn't a monster. He just didn't suffer guilt over what his wealth gave him. He enjoyed the rewards of his labour, and why not? All

---

1. Bravo.

she did was work, or think about getting work, and it never ended.

Tobias lifted a glass, his mop of hair dropped over one eye. "To Kerstin," he said. "For making me remember what it was like to be happy." She blushed. "*Prost.*"

"*Prost.*"

While they drank, Kerstin was glad they were all unapologetically ambitious, worked hard, and were distinctly unlike those who spend the bulk of their days sleeping off the dull aftertaste of overindulgence.

For days, *Deutschland* was the three of them on long walks near the Potsdamer Platz and the Brandenburger Tor. They ate *Kartoffeln. Bratwurst. Sauerkraut.* Drank *Bier.* Sat in restaurants among cold northerners and passionate southerners. Smoked hash from the Netherlands. Bartered with street vendors. Danced in clubs to house music. And on Shrove Tuesday, three weeks later, newlyweds Kerstin Ostheim-Vogel and Tobias Vogel sat in a limousine driving from the airport, embarking on a commitment to build a life together based on a calculation of compatibility made during a meeting at a press junket.

The couple leaned shoulder-to-shoulder, moved backwards in standard time, and their luggage jostled in the trunk as they were whisked away into tropical sunlight. In approximately fifty minutes, the newlyweds arrived at Tobias Vogel's home perched perilously on a mountain slope in Granger's Grove. They were deposited beside potted tropical plants in the driveway, and after the driver, wearing beige shorts, carried their bags to the front door, Kerstin wondered if, weather permitting, she'd spend the next morning writing beside the pool.

They walked a path bordered on both sides by fluffy blue hydrangeas.

At the door, Tobias kissed her before opening up. Then Kerstin followed him into a hallway lined with framed photographs of cityscapes at night, and into a living room with a wide window and a bird's-eye view of a sandy cove in the bottom of a valley.

Early days, there was a demand for organic toothpaste in the Asian market, so Tobias worked no fewer than fifty hours each week. It wasn't long before he had to travel to Bangkok for several weeks. While he was gone, Kerstin sat on the terrace with a view of waves splashing in the bay. Currents thrummed in her skull, and she didn't know whether to pop to the supermarket to top up on groceries or order in. She decided not to decide.

She settled in front of their flat-screen television to binge on DVDs of old Sonja Henie films. As she adjusted a pillow at her back for comfort, she felt narrow-minded for calling Tobias's world superficial (as she used to do when she stole toilet paper from public bathrooms).

On Tobias's return from his business trip, Kerstin found her opinion sought after over breakfast in matters related to interior decorating.

"Do you think the colour scheme in the kitchen matches the island at its apex?" he asked.

"It does," she replied. "But the major problem is the dark brown. It should be citrine."

"You think?"

"Uh-huh, and the *Badezimmer*[1] in the guest room should be furnished with kitschier magazines? *Architectural Digest* doesn't cut it," she said.

---

1. bathroom

Tobias wiped the mop of hair out his eyes. "Would you prefer marble tile at the front door?"

"God, yes!" She clutched his arm. "Green marble. Yes."

Soon she was involved in the hiring of a new housemaid, she made calls to have a new filter installed in the pool, and she was conscripted to replace the cityscapes in the hallway with "contemporary art that will accrue in value." And on a spontaneous retreat to a hotel with a miniature golf course, they made love on ivory sand before taking a dip among reefs studded with octopus and starfish.

The world intruded:

He was needed in Bangkok again.

Team Ostheim/Vogel Skyped over broken connections, they spoke saucily about their sexual fantasies with a strap-on, and made plans to spend another weekend in another hotel.

* * *

All that is good crumbles, so Kerstin wasn't blindsided when, imperceptibly at first, little by little, married life turned on Team Ostheim/Vogel much like it did with her parents, the governor and Mrs. Ostheim. Under the loosely defined terms of their marriage contract, Kerstin and Tobias found themselves hedged in by unwritten clauses pertinent to quality time. Therefore, over a Skype connection, Team Ostheim/Vogel vowed to make the first evening of his return from Bangkok an intimate dinner night at home, one Tobias playfully suggested would end with "a bang." Unfortunately, quality time together came at the expense of whatever moments Tobias needed to catch up on emails in his inbox on his arrival from the airport, and he joined Kerstin an hour and a half later than planned.

He sat opposite her at a varnished table in front of bowls filled with cold potato-leek soup. Then he launched into a lengthy explanation rather than an apology. "Are you upset?" he concluded.

"*Ne.*[1] I'm okay."

"Really?"

"*Ja*, just a bit tired is all. You?"

"Same." He swallowed a spoonful of soup. "We really ought to take a vacation. How's the Seychelles?"

"*Schön.*"[2]

It shouldn't have been so difficult to tell him, but she expected pushback. He'd ask her about her contraceptive pills, and by extension accuse her of not being careful enough. Sure, when they met he talked about family values and the importance of talking politics around the dinner table, but she had begun to see how much of what he said were words thrown around without any commitment behind them. Take his talk about a vacation; she knew it would fall by the wayside. There'd be scheduling conflicts. A conference in Tokyo. Unsatisfactory plane fares for desired dates. A crisis at the office in Bombay.

She got to the point. "I'm pregnant," she said.

"I thought we were being careful," he replied.

The pace at which everything swirled around Kerstin was so fast, holy fucking shit. She leaned on the edge of the kitchen counter, fighting waves of nausea. Suddenly, so much was changing, not inside her anymore but on the outside

---

1. No.
2. Nice.

now, and there seemed to be too much that was outside her control. He talked about "catastrophic timing." They were expanding their operations in Beijing, and a family wasn't something he could realistically do for at least two years. As Kerstin listened, she wondered if in a few months she'd look back at this moment and wish she had done something differently, and so she started talking and talking, and the severity of what she said about his selfishness shocked them both to no end.

"You're a fucking monster," she concluded. "A heartless, fucking monster."

After a long pause, he excused himself to go back to work.

* * *

1:36 p.m. After lunch with Jacquin, Kerstin walks the boulevard in darkly robust glasses, scrolling through information in her head about the recent horse fatalities. Schuld called to tell her about Woloff finding the foal's head, so she's on her way to the office to plot a way forward. Her breathing is filed down to the quick. She's on edge. What is she looking at? There have been five victims in the last week, but there's no reason she can think of why they're being slaughtered. She has to reread autopsy reports to see if she missed anything, and she'll need to phone horse ranches to see if anyone is losing mares to theft. Kerstin stops in her tracks to quickly jot down reminders and is happy they're not about the wedding. She needs to work more to feel her life has logic to it, otherwise she's thrown into a hotel of infinite rooms where mistakes she's made cling to every one of her thoughts.

It stinks of deranged weeds.

At the office, she calls a number of stables and tries to track down helpful leads.

"Hi, sweetie." Eion sits on her desk. "The sympathy card is in the mail."

"What? Why?"

He peers at the swirling psychedelic fractals infolding on her computer screen. "I heard your father is running for the last time."

"True."

"Good for him for knowing when to step aside," he replies, finally looking at her.

"I don't particularly know what he'll do with himself in retirement," she says. "He's happiest with projects to keep him occupied."

"You owe me some work, darling," Eion says.

"Oh." She thought they were talking about her dad. "I'll have it done by the weekend."

"The dead foal is a good focus for the story," Eion says. "Interview the parents of the cerebral palsy kid and talk to the OCU athlete."

"Woloff, I know him."

"They bring in the intersectionality I was talking to you about," he says. "We need to see the effect the decapitated head has on them as human beings."

"Sure," she replies.

First, she texts Schuld.

Will stop by gallery for opening tomorrow. So proud of you. Hope to see Woloff too. Mama. ♥

Then she phones the governor and leaves him a message. "Tag. You're it," she says. "I miss you. Call when you're able."

* * *

<u>5:02 p.m.</u> At the end of the day, Kerstin and P.J. are full of chit-chat over Americanos at a window of Café Hashim's. The day has been full, so they put it away by talking film.

"Everyone loves the cab scene," he says.

"No. No thanks." She refers to the scene in *Im Chor Der Engel Stehn* that helped Rita Oozol net a Prix d'interprétation féminine for her portrayal of Klara, a socialite addicted to raves and ecstasy. "Awful," Kerstin says. "Her meltdown went on for thirty minutes?"

P.J. cracks a smile. "It was five," he replies.

"It felt like thirty."

His phone rings and he answers it. "No, sir," he says. "No thanks."

"As a newlywed who bought flatware from our store, you're eligible for a discounted settee of your choice from Gingham's," says a man with traces of a West African accent. "With your offer, you get a free coffee table and a book with majestic photographs of the Dakotan Badlands. It all costs a one-time lowball total of $283 after taxes."

"I said, thank you no, sir."

"If you order now we can throw in the cost for transportation, but no later than the sixth of this month, as this is a one-time deal."

"Free transportation?"

"Yes, and if you provide us with your email, we can also send updates on all our latest offers. Here at Gingham's, we do the work, you enjoy the fruits of the labour."

"What grain of wood does that coffee table come in?"

Kerstin takes the phone from P.J. and hangs up.

"We don't need whatever he's selling, *Liebe*," she says. "Our credit cards are maxed."

Hashim interrupts to ask if they'll sample a dish he's experimenting with using ingredients fresh from the market. He places omelettes in front of them and hides out in the kitchen while they stare at a folded golden egg flap studded with cilantro. Their fork penetrates skin, squirting melted cheese. And after they secure morsels of cheesy egg, they slowly place them into their mouths and chew their way through gypsy mushrooms and chives.

Impatient to know what they think, Hashim hurries back. "You like?"

"I may never eat anyone else's omelette again," Kerstin says, hating the words as she speaks them.

"You've outdone yourself again, Hashim," P.J. adds.

Flattered, Hashim pesters them for one of P.J.'s headshots of Kerstin for his wall, row upon row of framed and signed photographs of celebrities who have visited his café—a long list of feathery plumed hoofers from Broadway, and singers whose brushes with fame have been parlayed into autograph signings in malls.

"I'm not famous," she says.

"You're the governor's daughter." He follows her on Twitter. "Of course you're famous."

After Hashim leaves them, Kerstin tries to tell P.J. something she doesn't quite have the words for. "Did I ever tell you that I may be the messiest person when it comes to the household and paying bills and eating regularly and healthily, but that I go crazy when all the thoughts in my head stop being perfectly organized and logical? Whenever I lose control over my head, I get very nervous—and a little excited and happy at the same time, strangely enough—and smoke too much and fidget around and bite my fingernails." She fidgets as though to demonstrate. "What I'm saying is that there are things about you I don't know ahead of our marriage, and it makes me nervous."

"Like?"

"Does it matter to you that your father's white?"

"I'm white too," he replies.

"Yes, but you're also Indigenous."

"Yes," he replies. "But that doesn't make me not white as well."

"Okay. Then you have no beef with him about his attempt to keep his land on the east side."

"None of that has to do with his race," he replies.

She's baffled. "That's difficult to believe."

"Fuckfuck."

"What?"

"I was supposed to drop off multivitamins for Pop this morning." He gathers his car keys from the table. "Shitshit. I can't fuck up again."

"It's not a big deal," Kerstin says.

"I can't mess up." He kisses her forehead. "We'll finish this talk later."

* * *

6:05 p.m. A Janus cat is born with two faces, and action must be taken, right away.

At Pop's front door, Gixx leaps onto P.J. with his paws. P.J. carefully lowers them to the floor and gets on a knee as the dog rushes around him, licking his ears.

121

"Nice to see you too," he says.

Gixx flops down beside him, exposing his underbelly for P.J. to scratch.

"Anyone home?" he calls out.

"Bedroom," Pop replies.

"I gotta check in on the old man," P.J. murmurs to the dog.

In the bedroom, Matilda spoons creamy formula into P.J. Sr.'s mouth. She wipes him clean with a wet cloth, making sure his nostrils are clear.

"What happened?" P.J. asks.

"Where were you?" Pop replies.

"Work stuff," P.J. says.

"The medication makes my hands numb," Pop replies. "The doctor says it might be a day or two before I adjust."

"I can get that," P.J. says, handing Matilda a bag of multivitamins and taking the spoon from her.

On her way out, she turns on a ceiling fan, redistributing the muggy, stiff air with whirring blades, and P.J. scoops baby formula into his father's mouth.

They've been getting along, and neither one of them wants misunderstandings that lead to arguments.

After Pop has eaten, he can't stop talking. He speaks about iceboxes used to store food after the Great Depression and describes when groceries were delivered by horseback on Fridays (or Thursdays, he doesn't remember). His head of pepper-white hair bobs as his brain lurches with juiced neurotransmitters, and he changes directions again. This time his focus is on diction and grammar and how people don't know the difference between *lay* and *lie*. "What about the ones who use *me* in a sentence that begins *me and him*? Only the donkey would name itself first." During his stay in the hospital he watched the game show *A.I.*, an hour-long competition in which a panel of artificial intelligence judges choose winners of a former-child-celebrity spelling bee, and it sets off in Pop a chain of ideas about being virtual and present all at the same time, and ends with Einstein boiling his watch instead of eggs because he was such an absent-minded genius. And he can't stop unpacking ideas from their wrapping as he crackles along on pink oval pills. He segues into a tangent on the miracle that is pods of larvae and finally returns to what he remembers of his original point. "Don't get married, P.J.!" he concludes.

"Why would you say that, Pop?"

"She's divorced."

"Yes," he replies. "And she has a daughter who happens to be transgender. So?"

"A what?"

"Transgender daughter."

"Oh, son," Pop replies. "Don't take on the problems of a divorcee with a transvestite child."

"Transgender, Pop," P.J. corrects.

"Transwhatever. That sort of complicated relationship requires a level of stability you don't yet have. You mustn't bite off more than you can chew."

P.J. feels like a goon has stuck a plastic bag over his head. He's suffocating. Except it all takes place in his brain, like a play. This is the first time he recollects when he has thought, good, he has everything he wanted, and he's content. He isn't thinking about what else there is and what other little surprises life still has to offer. Good Lord, he refuses to become like his morally judgmental father and retreat into an endless expanse of not bad, mostly quite okay, sometimes happy, sometimes sad—and somehow just never enough. P.J.'s legs shake uncontrollably as he stares at Pop without much feeling, a territoriless prince rejecting all tokens of his father's affection.

He wants to pee. His mind closes.

10 Days to Wedding

<u>11:03 a.m.</u> It's the morning after the comet appeared. Clothes are draped over milk crates in his bedroom while a naked Woloff rests his head on Schuld's belly, a porcelain plain that ends in a vista of bush.

"Don't think you're forgiven for flaking out on me last night," Woloff says.

"I was inspired."

"You could have sent me a text."

"I'm sorry, baby," she says. "I thought you'd understand."

"I worried about you."

"It won't happen again," she replies.

He grouses. "I worry."

"I really am sorry," she says. "How are you dealing?"

"Better since you stopped by." They had talked until the songbirds welcomed the dawn. "I'm not obsessively thinking about the foal and questioning everything that happened with Rick."

"We can talk more if you want," she says.

"No need," he replies. "Today is all about your art opening."

His phone dingles, and he sits up against a pillow to read a text from Precious.

Rafiki,[1] I'm happy to announce my engagement to Eric Jones (a lawyer with the International Development Organization (IDO)). Cheers.

Attached is a JPEG of his ex wrapped in the arms of a bespectacled brother in front of a tent at the base of Mount Kilimanjaro. For reasons better explained by a therapist, Woloff fixates on Eric's hand tucked snugly under Precious's elbow.

Oh, wait. Schuld jumps from one cluster of ideas to the next, trying to find a fit for what she feels so she can lapse back into quietude. It's like ironing out wrinkles in cotton. She has a plan to divert the Nile River from the southern into the northern Sudan, thereby turning the desert into arable land. Soon she is talking about money, and of her estranged father's deep pockets, and how her mother won't take money from him, even with her modest income. She hates money "unless it's a tool" to get the only thing she needs, the financing to divert the Nile River from the southern into the northern Sudan.

"How lucky you were to have grown up with parents who had a modest income," Woloff replies, shutting off his phone.

"Lucky? How?" Schuld asks, pulling him down next to her.

"I was born after the salad days. The ones where our family lost its land in the locust infestation of '73." He stares into her differently coloured eyes. "I never had the luxury to hate money the way you do."

---

1. Comrade

Schuld laughs. "*Du spaßvogel.*"[2] Her fingers play along his ear, meandering, full of bop, into his tangled hair. "Are we still cool about my painting Demarion?" she asks.

He's going to be an installation piece roaming around the gallery nude at the opening tonight.

"We cool," he says, trying to convince himself.

"Really?" she asks.

"Of course, bae," he replies. "I encourage it. It's art. That shit has to be real."

She drapes a leg over his backside before digging thumbs into his upper back to search for knots. "How's the leg this morning?"

"Fucked," he says.

"Are you leaning toward surgery?"

"Yup," he replies. "It's the long-term solution."

"Jesus!" she says. "It would also end your college career."

"That might not be such a bad thing," he says. "I haven't run well in years. I need to move on."

As the breeze rustle the curtains, Woloff talks about the foal and how it reminds him of the man he watched taken from the bus at gunpoint. Schuld recollects the night her arm was broken, and the sense of terror she experienced during her recent assault. They agree. These separate moments vary in their violence, but are similar in how they've left their bodies. Dissipated. Deflated. Their minds sorting through jumbles of stupidity. Why the fuck? Why the fuckity fuck? And since they no longer believe in definitive explanations for violence's variations, they don't quite know where to put themselves.

---

1. You joker.

* * *

<u>12:18 p.m.</u> They pool their cash before trundling off to the grocery store to restock Woloff's fridge.

He pushes the cart while she decides what to put in.

"We need to find a mayo with less calories," she says. "And the tuna...get the one in water, not oil."

"Not oil?" he asks.

"Not oil, yes," she replies.

In the aisle with the dairy products, she playfully kisses around a canary-yellow circle powdered onto his chin.

A gym rat with oiled biceps steps in front of their shopping cart. "I'm college-educated," he announces.

"Congratulations," Schuld replies.

"Is that sarcasm?" he asks.

"No," Schuld says. "I'm glad for you."

"I'm not some schmo," he replies.

"Can you...move?" Woloff says. "We can't get past."

"Hold up!" The gym rat places a hand on the cart, staring at his yellow chin. "I'm no snowflake."

Woloff reverses, pulling Schuld with him by the hand.

"I'm college-educated," the gym rat shouts at them as they head for the cash register.

They get lit at Woloff's and then wander around downtown, plugged into an iPod that plays Dr. Dre's *Chronic*. Their hands are crammed into one another's back pockets as they mill about on a street clogged with people who've been flushed out of rooms like rats from a sewer, and they keep a look out for the hostility of those who don't tolerate the miscellaneous doings of dongs with other dongs. In lockstep, they pass a store window cluttered with objects that will accrue in sentimental value—trinkets, goblets, and pictures of fighter bombers and soldiers hugging sweethearts in airports. Then they stop at the front door of the sHipley Art Gallery.

"Break a leg," he says.

"Laterz," she replies.

* * *

4:17 p.m. Demarion stands in front of Schuld while she paints his penis, carefully slathering it turquoise.

"I need a job where I don't get bitten by the boss's dog," Schuld says.

"Would you waitress in a bar?"

"*Ja*," Schuld says. "It can't be too different from working in a restaurant. I've done that."

"There's an opening at work," he says. "With tips you take home two bones a night. Easy."

"Awesomesauce," Schuld replies, stepping back to admire her handiwork. Then she drags out a wooden crate, steps on it, and begins to paint his face mustard-yellow.

"Your eyes." His breath is hot and sour against her chin. "They don't... Hold on." He steps away to grab a candle from a side table. Then he trains its flickering light about two inches from her nose. "Right there." Schuld blinks. "They're two different colors."

"Yours aren't too bad either," she replies.

He stands in front of her again. "Weird!" he says.

"I've got heterochromia," she says.

"They're quite bizarre," he replies.

* * *

8:29 p.m. Of late, unruly imaginings have had their way with Woloff. True story, he's upset the Sunderlands won't let him stop by to say a proper goodbye to Rick. He likes him and values the progress they made in the past year. They communicated by making faces, changing the tones of their voices, and using a variety of hand signals they invented together. How little this bond mattered to his parents frustrates him. He has a hit of sativa, then preoccupies himself by composing a text to Schuld. It's her big night. He congratulates her again, sends her positive vibes, and concludes with an aside about celebratory festivities that call attention to his black c**k in the vicinity of her white a*s.

He regrets it as soon as he sends it.

It was supposed to be tongue-in-cheek. It was supposed to be a joke, not an oozing pimple on the butt of interracial romance. Dammit. There's no pathway to redemption. The only appropriate time to acknowledge race is for the collection of a census. Thus, as Woloff walks sHipley Art Gallery's hallway, he readies to explain himself and clarify his intentions to Schuld.

Walls hung with canvases splattered with multicoloured polka dots surround him as he negotiates thin Giacometti-like bronze sculptures randomly set up on the hardwood floor. Around him in a room glancing with fluorescent lights, people sip from beer bottles or plastic cups while they shout at one another over the loud thump of a house track. A hand touches his shoulder, and he turns to see Kerstin, in a plaid dress and wearing horn-rimmed glasses.

"Did you just get here?" she asks.

Woloff points to his ears.

She leans into one ear. "Can we talk?" she asks.

Woloff nods.

"As you've heard from Schuld, I'm writing an article on the horse killings, and I wondered if I could interview you about the foal you found at the beach."

"I don't think that's a good idea." He lowers his voice because he can't tell if he's yelling. "I was working under the table."

"Oh!"

"The track coach got me the job after I got injured my sophomore year because I was losing sponsorships," he says. "The Sunderlands are members of his church, and it was a favour they did for him."

"I didn't know...well, any of these things about you," she replies. "Schuld says so little."

"Have you talked to the Sunderlands?"

"Not yet."

"They probably don't want the attention," he replies. "I'm sorry I can't help."

"No," she says. "It's perfectly fine."

"Wanna drink?" Woloff asks. "I wouldn't mind grabbing a beer before I take in the exhibit."

"I'm good," she says. "P.J. is somewhere around here. Find us later. We'll make plans for the four of us to spend time together after the wedding."

"Fersurely," Woloff replies.

He heads to a table stocked with beer in bowls of ice, helps himself to a can of Guinness, and goes up back stairs into a hallway of studios. Schuld's is three doors down, where he finds her sitting on the floor taking hits off a pipe with the giant mustard-yellow-and-turquoise installation piece, Demarion Armstrong. He spits a rap about relaxing and about true lovers freewheeling it sans undies in travelling vans.

"Baby!" Schuld exclaims.

"I can explain," Woloff says.

"S'up, man," Demarion interjects.

"Did Mutti find you?" she asks.

"We just talked," Woloff says. "Did you get my text?"

"I haven't checked my phone in a while," she says. "I've been sorta busy."

"Erase it," he says.

She hands him the pipe. "Now I really wanna see it."

They're interrupted at the door by a request for Demarion's and Schuld's presence downstairs for the opening-ceremony speech.

* * *

11:46 p.m. Woloff's knee gives out on him while he's parked beside the booze table, so he has to make it an early night. Not that this is a problem for him. Yes, he appreciates art, and Schuld's repurposed doodads and her reinterpretation of their meanings made him think about how he's touched by bits and pieces of the different places he's been. Her motley collection of misfit objects woke in him an unwillingness to keep thinking about his peculiarities in ways that make him struggle in the mornings to open the curtains and let the sunlight in.

That said, he didn't know what to make of Demarion Armstrong roaming the gallery in the nude all night. He was art, or had become it, something of the sort, and that was all good. Unfortunately though, his spontaneous bursts of inspired krumping were...strange.

* * *

On returning home, Woloff's much too tired to do anything except crawl into bed. Under the blanket he can't get comfortable. His pillow is much too fluffy. His knee bellyaches. And in the living room Bill Tilson, his roommate, argues with Jim Wilts, the steeplechaser.

"Motherfucker."

"You're the motherfucker."

"I was waiting half an hour."

"It was ten minutes at the most."

"Lying motherfucker."

Feet stomp, fists smackthud, bodies tumble to the floor. There's crashing furniture. A door slams. Pots clang against the floor. Schuld reappears in queasiness that burbles up in Woloff's solar plexus. She didn't mention the text when she put him in a cab, and he'd been in too much pain to think about asking her about it. He pops a Perc. Then he quietly waits for the fighting to stop and for his mind to empty. What did Namunyuk mean that she saw no future? Could it be his track career? He places his book on the bedside table, switches off his lamp, shuts his eyes, and waits for sleep, unaware of when it'll come, like death.

9 Days to Wedding

<u>9:07 a.m.</u> In the morning, Woloff groggily boils a couple of eggs and eats them in bed while reading online message boards that point out what is wrong with other people. After smoking a bowl and chasing it down with another Perc, he makes an appointment at the dentist far enough into the future so he doesn't have to think about how meaningless it is to take a time-consuming bus ride and sit in a waiting room with a magazine in order to listen to all the costly things he'll need done to maintain the health of his decaying molars. He gussies up with makeup before checking his phone for a message from Schuld. Nothing again. He needs to keep preoccupied.

He takes the #14 bus to PHIL 427—Realist Philosophy with Professor Akzlow—at 11:00 a.m. in room 514. Twenty-five minutes later he's on campus, and five after that he's walked across shorn grass to the fifth floor of the Rontaka-heen Building. Chop, chop. Woloff hops to it. Jacked on caffeine, his right brain is provoked by students in a corridor, scrums of folk who sputter into view, shape-shifting.

There are twenty registered students in the class, but on

any given day attendance hovers between four and twelve. He gets comfy in the back with a view of Professor Akzlow, wearing an ankle-length woollen skirt and Doc Marten boots, standing in front of a PowerPoint, a sepia pic of a labyrinth on the screen behind her. In the middle of the room, beside the window, sits Max Zinfandel in a Nirvana T-shirt, and at desks at the front wait Dak Temle in crimson sweats and Ola Palea, as always, poised to scratch notes into their exercise books.

Professor Akzlow clicks onto a pic of Rita Oozol in sunglasses with huge round frames, pushing a shopping cart through the parking lot of a supermarket. "What can you tell me about her?"

"She kinda sorta an OCU alum," Dak says.

"The first actor from the Cove to win an Emmy," Max adds.

"She got a kid," Olivia says. "So she's a working mother."

"You've all identified her by categories," Professor Akzlow says. "However, what does our short list really tell us about her?"

"How she appears as phenomenon or whatever?" Olivia offers.

"With her dope exotic snakes," Dak says.

"Saying 'chop, chop' all the time," Woloff chimes in.

"Yes, this idea of her is what we take, in an act of Sartrean bad faith, to be real," Professor Akzlow says. "There's no separation between our idea, its sensory impression, and the object it refers to." She clicks onto a slide of a drawing of a brain. "What other ways can we think about Rita Oozol?"

"She's driven," Dak says.

"And nice, or whatever, with all her work with reptiles," Olivia adds. "She has an iguana, and chameleons. Then she gave—what was it?—a quarter of a million dollars to the crocodile preservation foundation thing."

"Yes, her intentions manifest in how she appears in our various encounters with her," Professor Akzlow replies. "What we know about her is tethered to what we see. And our habits of thinking, full of gaps, produce what we determine is this knowledge." She stops to drink a glass of water. "Once upon a while ago the unconscious was a form of theatre—the lead playing out their genealogical determinants. Hamlet grapples to avenge his father's death, and it's the role of the parents that's imagined as what psychologically shapes who we become." She clicks on a slide of a tree. "Adherents to this old model of thought believe objectivity is received truth."

"This reminds me of our discussion about threshold moments, or whatever." Olivia looks down at her notes from last week, her free hand holding aside hair that threatens to drop over her eyes. "They rupture our ideas with their overcoding morality composed of absolute truths guaranteed by God, correct?"

"Yes," the professor says. "In the absence of the Absolute, the new emerges."

"Everything is translated through a lens, or whatever," Olivia says. "Like how we relate to Rita Oozol. We've gotten rid of the idea that there's anything real to hold on to."

"Can you make that good point by returning to how Descartes's essay grapples with your idea?" Professor Akzlow asks. "Sorry, Deleuze. Gilles Deleuze. Did I say Descartes? Big difference. I meant... You know what I meant."

Woloff checks his phone for a message from Schuld. Nada. He's irritated with himself for the damn text, and wonders whether any of the ideas they're discussing in class will help him better explain himself to her. He could tell her that his words weren't his meaning. What he meant wasn't what the words made of it. He could say he needs her to see this in order to exist in the world of fact.

"Any questions so far?" Professor Akzlow asks.

So it goes for another hour, and after class, there's a buzz of chit-chat as Woloff deposits his papers and books into his backpack, trying to remember a quote from the reading about deterritorializing. Max talks with Professor Akzlow, trying to clarify a point he made about Rita Oozol as a simulacrum, and Dak gives Olivia an encouraging pep talk full of ingredients for a recipe for a life well-lived. Exposure to vitamin D from the sun. Pot. Chop, chop, Woloff thinks as he walks out the door.

* * *

<u>1:42 p.m.</u> A numinous experience is what he seeks, not reassurance, and since faith without deeds is bogus, he tells himself that he won't check his phone more than once every fifteen minutes. He does maintenance-type tasks at home that involve no deep knee bends (and leave him with a relatively satisfying sense of überproductivity). He wipes walls down and replaces the hinges on the cabinet beneath the sink. Afterwards, he takes a broom to cobwebs while daydreaming of late-night dips in kidney-shaped Jacuzzis.

The phone rings.

"*Unaweza kuongea?*"[1] It's Precious.

"Not long," Woloff replies.

---

1. Can you talk?

Precious redirects to Eric, who's in the vicinity. "He can't talk long," she says.

Eric shouts in the background. "Tell him..." There's a shuffle of papers. "No, give me the phone.... Woloff. What up? It's Eric."

"Hey."

"I just wanted to introduce myself right quick," he says. "I'm a big fan. I watched you finish third in the 1,500 at the Olympics your freshman year. Gutsy race. You led until the final forty metres."

"I try not to remember the last part," Woloff replies.

"I look forward to meeting you."

"Me too."

Precious gets back on the line. "I'm glad you got to say hey to Eric," she says. "He's impressed I know you."

"I really do have to go."

"One thing about the trans woman before you split."

"Her name's Schuld," he replies.

"Are you sure you know what you're doing?"

"Of course I do."

"Be careful," she says, satisfied in this solid advice from good, solid people.

What the fuck! "I'll keep that in mind," he replies.

The afternoon passes dully, and Woloff still hasn't heard from Schuld. He knows she's busy prepping for another show, so he doesn't want to bug her. However, he ignores logic—it doesn't make sense—gives in to his impulses, and goes to sHipley's early, unannounced.

Schuld won't let him in. Instead, they stand in the gallery's doorway.

"Are you here to tap this white ass?" she asks.

"About that..."

"*Ja.*"

"It was like, y'know when you're thinking out loud," Woloff says. "It was like that. Just ideas. And I was trying to suggest that, generally speaking...what's wrong with acknowledging racial markers? Not as the whole of desire, but as a part of it." He isn't satisfied with his explanation. "I'm sorry for offending you."

"No offence taken," she replies. "It was...saucy."

"You think?"

"And hilarious," she replies.

"Can you take a short break?" he asks.

"Not right now," she says.

"Schuld!" It's Demarion in the background. "Are you coming?"

Woloff makes out the 7-foot-8 giant sitting on a crate in the middle of the exhibition space. He's naked, covered from head to toe in turquoise and mustard paint.

"I've got to get, *Schatz*," Schuld says. "Demarion's going through stuff."

"The krumping?"

She chuckles. "Come back in an hour," she says. "It'd be cool to get away from the gallery before the show."

She returns inside and locks the door behind her.

* * *

4.33 p.m. Off the F-3 highway, Woloff and Schuld descend a path that emerges on a rickety bridge that crosses above a surging stream. Gingerly, Woloff tests a rotting plank with a foot, then he carefully steps forward.

"Don't pinch my ass," he says.

Schuld grabs at a paperback poking out of his back pocket.

"Do you really want me to lose focus out here?" Woloff brushes her hand away and keeps moving along wood that creaks beneath them. "My leg's wonky."

Once they're on the other side of the bridge, they dismount onto a path overgrown with guinea grass that leads into a bay where waves rush an inlet in which small groups of children bob in the water. Further out, snorkels stick out of water in front of a pod of surfers who wait for a set to lift them up, curl over them, and splash them in the mid-afternoon heat. Woloff and Schuld walk loose sand beside a flat promontory of dark rock that disappears and then reappears in a wash of waves. Then they settle on a spot as far away as possible from those who stare out at the sea, dressed in vintage swim cuts, adrift on thoughts modulated by water that surges at the shore.

Woloff lights a spliff. Schuld smears her arms and legs with sunscreen. As the glare of a sun drops on the eastern horizon, they sit on a towel and lean against one another in the shade of a princess palm, finally not being rushed.

Woloff puffs vape smoke from a pen out his nostrils. "Do you think we can know other people?"

"We can't know anyone totally, but we can understand them partially," she replies.

"Is that enough?"

"It can be," she replies. "Try it. Ask away."

"Tell me something about yourself I don't know."

"I'm an open book," she says.

"You're stalling."

"C'mon, Woloff," she says. "Help me a little. I need a specific question, like...where did you get that scar?"

He points at her shin. "Where did you get that scar?"

Schuld has a pull of weed before she hands the vape pen

back to him. "When I was a kid my parents walked around the house naked sometimes. I can't even recall when I first learned about sex because all those body parts and what you could do with them were never a secret. Then one day when I was in the third grade, a few boys were running around the schoolyard during break, pulling down each other's shorts. I thought they were so stupid and I became really annoyed, so when everyone settled down for art class after the break, I stood up next to my chair, pulled down my pants, and yelled at them, 'Is that what you all want to see so badly?!' I can still see my classmates' faces and then all the shouting and giggling and pointing, while one student ran outside to tell the teacher. After class, she asked me to stay behind and sat me down, and I felt so humiliated because I had never gotten into trouble at school before. I had always been a quiet, shy kid. Then she explained to me how what I had done was so wrong, and how it would reflect badly on the whole school if any of the other students told their parents what I'd done. I was so ashamed. It felt as though everyone thought I was totally depraved. I ran out of the class and into the hallway and tripped on someone's backpack. I wound up with fifteen stitches in my shin." She picks up a handful of sand before letting it dribble through her fingers. "Looking back, I want to laugh about it because I remember that feeling of shame too well, and I still blush on thinking about it.

"That feeling was one of the reasons I left home when I was sixteen. It was just Mutti and me, and neither one of us was doing that great. Papi's organic toothpaste company had been on blast for exploiting cheap labour in factories in the Asian market, so she stopped taking alimony payments from his 'blood money.' I knew I was a girl, but I didn't know how to make my outside match my inside. This meant we were fighting all the time over stupid shit and I felt really bad about myself all the time. Something had to change. The day I finally decided to leave, I packed a canvas bag full of clothes, left a note on the kitchen table for Mutti, and let myself out the back door. Later that night, I was walking the Cove without a clue where I was going to sleep. Stores were still open, late-nighters popping in and out for potato chips." She rubs the Band-Aid on her shoulder. "I carried my canvas bag until I reached Denturra Beach Park, scaled the iron gate, and set up shop on a bench inside. Once I'd settled, I yanked my sleeping bag up to my chin.

"The odd pedestrian walked around me, and I held on to a penknife I'd use if anyone bothered me. When a gust of wind knocked a garbage bin out square against the cement and spilled metal cans onto the walkway, I didn't think I'd get through the night.

"I lived under a bridge near the park for a month. I'd go through garbage cans, looking for butts with smokable stubs and for food that didn't smell like it was well past its expiry date. I washed my body in the sink of public bathrooms and cleaned my underwear in water fountains. Then I looked over the classifieds for job openings in restaurants and on construction sites. *Nichts.*[1] Finally, desperate enough, I bumped into a man with a briefcase on the subway and lifted a money clip from his jacket pocket. One hundred and sixty dollars richer, I binged on cheeseburgers at McDonald's before going back to the bridge. I ended up getting a job as a waitress at a restaurant looking for an emergency hire and had a knack for remembering orders at tables with-

---

1. Nothing.

out scribbling details into a notebook. I had my own money collected in tips from customers I enjoyed bantering with. Soon I had moved into my own place, set up an easel, and, bolstered by mugginess caused by a faulty air conditioner, I painted abstractions of a girl who no longer felt hemmed in mundane content."

"Okay, that's a lot of somethings I didn't know about you," Woloff says.

Schuld rubs an eyeball with her palm. "What about you?"

"Wait!"

"No stalling."

"What do you want to partially understand?" he asks.

"What does Precious say about you in her book?" she asks.

"Not much," he says. "She focuses on the day-to-day of being a part of the insurgency. Raids. Camaraderie. Eating chocolate bars. Stuff."

"What little does she say about you?"

"She mentions an incident on my final night at home," he replies.

"Final night," she replies. "You mean, like a sexual incident."

"No, no," he says. "She describes a bonfire we had with a couple of her friends."

"What happened?"

He takes a spliff out of a zip-lock bag and lights up. "Shadrack Mejooli was this seventeen-year-old who left the village. He joined the mercenaries who'd been raiding farms in the area, looking for insurgents. One day, he showed up on my uncle Phineas's land with another soldier, and forced us to kneel in front of them with our hands on our heads. My uncle had a coop full of chickens, and he offered them as many as they wanted if they'd leave us alone.

"As we lay face first in the dirt, Shadrack and his friend helped themselves to chickens from the coop, stomped all over the vegetable garden, and, on leaving, knocked down part of a fence. A couple of days later I found out Shadrack died in a car crash.

"I'm usually skeptical about...well, just about everything. However, Namunyak, the witch doctor, claimed it happened the day after he pulled out the boma root she put on the grave of his father.

"That night, my last night in the country, Precious and I piled into the back of a dented truck with her pals Daniel Lemashon and Hannah Liloe. The four of us rattled over potholes on a road used by the big-wheeled trucks of a company building a huge dam in the area. Daniel drove us through miles of sugarcane fields until we arrived at Magogo Forest. Then we entered a backroad dense with deciduous trees and drove to a small clearing. Daniel pulled over to the side of the road and shut off the lights. We piled out before walking with flashlights to an abandoned lime quarry where monkeys jibber-jabbered in the trees.

"At the centre of the clearing, Hannah played posthumous Tupac on a boom box. Then we lit branches and dried grass with matches, and sat beside the bonfire with some home-made brew. We sparked up some herb and talked about how Precious and company had been stealing guns from camps of soldiers near the border. Soon we got around to the subject of Shadrack Mejooli's death.

"Precious said they fucked with his brakes after I told her what he did to my uncle and me, and that's how he died. I got angry, calling them murderers. They cracked up and said they were joking.

"I didn't know what to believe. Precious tried to convince

145

me that they had nothing to do with it. But I wasn't sure. Before I could press her on it, we heard distant engines revving on the road. Mercenaries had been patrolling the area looking for insurgents, so Hannah got us all rifles from a bag in the car, and Precious pushed a small box of bullets into my hand.

"The rumbling moved closer, and she led us into the bush with flashlights. We filed through branches until we stopped at the base of an umbrella tree. Precious hauled herself, one branch at a time, toward thicker leaves high above the ground. Then everyone else followed. I went last, misstepped on a branch, and I dropped about six feet, twisting my knee. Pain flared up around my kneecap as I climbed after them to a flat piece of plywood tied down with frayed ropes.

"It was a tight squeeze. Daniel and Hannah loaded the rifles, and then we all lay down with our guns trained on the darkness below us. I could feel my knee swell in my temples, and it was only a matter of time before the convoy of mercenaries stopped near the quarry. A few minutes later, floodlights appeared beside the smoking ashes at the firepit, and our abandoned bottles were shattered. Twigs snapped. Flashlights poked the foliage. Then Precious showed me a knife blade, pointed to Daniel, and they descended toward a couple of soldiers standing beneath us.

"As Precious and Daniel lowered themselves down the tree, there were gunshots deeper in the forest. So the two mercenaries hurried away toward the outbreak of noise."

"Jesus, Woloff," Schuld says.

"Precious lived in a whole other dimension." Woloff takes another pull from the joint. "I was nervous around her all the time, always expecting the worst to happen. That's nothing to be nostalgic about. The only thing I still have from that relationship is a fucked-up knee."

"Is the part about Shadrack Mejooli in the book?" Schuld asks.

"Nope," he replies. "But she does mention it's how I injured my knee."

In the cool of dusk, red buoys clomp up and down in water as everything prickles on the surface of their skin. Woloff crushes the butt into the sand, and they face each other. Then, against all that's holy, they angle their heads a little and kiss with tender ferocity before touching each other's forbidden parts.

* * *

6:24 p.m. Night creeps up on Ka'alipo Beach as Woloff picks fragments of shells from the sand, and gusts of breeze stir waves where Schuld floats next to a cement pipe embedded in the shallow water. She anchors herself by digging her elbows in the sand, and she waits for a large wave to wash over her before it recedes back into the ocean. An abrupt jerk of the undercurrent drags her beneath the surface. She fights to get to her feet, but another wave knocks her backward against the pipe. Her shoulder smacks cement. Another rush of water twirls her and deposits her back-first against jagged coral. Pain flushes through her body, and she swallows salty water that bubbles around her in foam.

When Woloff pulls Schuld from the ocean, he can hear the sky turn black.

* * *

11:12 p.m. At home, Schuld lies on her side in bed, Band-Aids patching cuts on her collarbone, back, waist, and both legs. She didn't make it to the gallery tonight. She's been pieced together at the emergency while answering queries from a doctor in green scrubs about whether she's on hormone replacement medication, and if she's interested in pamphlets with counselling options for people like her. Now there's a ruckus in her head, and she waits in the dark, held together by gravity and adhesive tape. As she listens to music on her iPod, she's a monk she once saw in a film reel who beat himself with sticks, unable to master a routine that encourages sleep. For an interval she hovers between the rustle of cymbals, feeling like a mosquito taken apart by hind limbs, and for an eternity she thinks of chewing the petals of purple carnations until ragas announce the slate-grey dawn. Runs of congas from an African bazaar bleating in her headphones with pleas too much for her eardrums.

She reaches over to the dresser for a bottle of water, but doubles over, cramping in the upper abdomen. She waits out the worst of it, her breath catching sharply on another secret she has to keep. If she mentions it to her mother, it will end up in the argument over what she needs to do to be healthy.

Her mind piles up with botched blueprints of how to get from here to there, and the air shakes chimes that whistle across plastic chairs heaped outside in a neighbourhood of backyards. In pain, she stares at her alarm clock, thinking about cars that roam the roads along Cove's tipsy shoreline. On the hour, she hears the bang of a gong from a temple, and she thinks of Urgroßvater as a woman living as a man with Urgroßmutter. It's a topic no one in the family discusses in depth. From what Schuld's gathered, the couple stayed together despite other people's judgments that supposedly came from a well-intentioned place and yet brought hostility. How did they manage to find the courage to be together back in the 1930s? Was it worth the personal cost? Did they grow bitter? What about Urgroßvater—when did he begin to understand he was different? Schuld had been too young to ask them these questions when they were alive, so it took years before she asked the people around her. Oma wouldn't talk about them, and Mutti didn't remember enough significant details to help Schuld get past what she already knew. Now the absence of her great-grandparents is a limit she can't overcome.

She sits up on her pillow, but muscles at her collarbone pinch around her windpipe. Therefore, she lies on her stomach and wishes to begin again with Woloff, beyond the mountains stacked on the city's perimeter—past macadamia nut plantations—in a place with caterpillars that spin silk cocoons on trees in the garden.

8 Days to Wedding

<u>12:05 a.m.</u> For the fourth time that night, Kerstin looks in on Schuld and then sidles up next to P.J. on the living room couch. She can't relax as they rewatch the TiVoed first episode of season 13 of *Switcher*, so she gets up for a fifth time to see if her daughter is still breathing.

"Take 'er easy!" P.J. says when she returns to snuggle against him on the couch. "It'll be fine."

Kerstin winces.

She would "take 'er easy," but look what happened when she left P.J. alone with Schuld. She trusted him to keep an eye on her while she adjusted to a higher dose of the Ramazipan, but he didn't do it properly. Hasn't she learned anything from her previous marriage? Tobias Vogel talked a good game, but fell short on follow-through. She reminds herself that she and P.J. agree that a relationship involves the kind of openness to another person's differences that facilitates mutual growth, and that they both believe a marriage should function like a winning team, without any egotistical stars. However, despite this bottom line, P.J. won't take her concerns seriously.

"It isn't fine," she says. "Just look at her."

"It will be fine," P.J. replies. "He's a…"

"She, not he," Kerstin interjects.

"Sorry," he says. "She's a healthy adult who'll bounce back quickly. You just have to let her be."

Kerstin sits up. "She's not your average nineteen-year-old," she says. "She ended up in a hospital when I wasn't more involved in her life."

"What happened at the beach was an accident," he replies.

Kerstin flushes at her neckline. "Things have been looking up for her lately," she says. "So a setback is a big deal." There's more to it, of course. She didn't have a problem with Schuld's transformation, but it wasn't expected. Her son is now her daughter, and she really doesn't have a problem with it. Truly. She loves her to pieces. That's what matters, not what gender she is. The difficulty lies in that she always has to be ready for the unexpected. There's always more uncertainty with Schuld, not less, and it never ends.

"It *is* a big deal." P.J. reaches for her hand, and she struggles not to pull it away from him. "But let's talk about this in the morning after some sleep. Everything will be less overwhelming."

She's heard similar words before from Tobias, but Kerstin reminds herself that P.J. isn't her ex-husband. She's grown up a lot in the past decade. She survived a divorce, made a difficult decision to be close to Schuld during her tumultuous coming-out period, and she's finally making a name for herself as an investigative journalist. Now that she's turned her attention to sharing this growth with another person, she has to make sure she doesn't revert to the person she used to be. Therefore, she breathes in and out through her nose before nudging up against P.J. to focus on *Switcher*.

In this episode, Sonja (Tamala Exeter) meets Anastasia (Rita Oozol) at the vet clinic, where she takes her Labrador to deal with a broken bone in his paw. However, the lovers-to-be get off on the wrong foot when they get into an angry exchange at the front desk. Sonja's Lab is in pain, and she doesn't want to wait half an hour to get him some relief. Anastasia has other dog patients, including one with a fractured jaw. She can't get to it "chop, chop." As their argument escalates, Kerstin's mood sours. She can't accept the veterinarian's lack of empathy, and she wonders whether P.J.'s lackadaisical approach is similarly out of touch. She wants to be open to his laissez-faire approach to life and respect his need to keep things to himself, but his attitude makes her worry all the time.

* * *

<u>1:21 a.m.</u> Outside, a steady rain kicks up and falls in large drops garbling in storm drains. In the bathroom, P.J. swishes a minty antibiotic around in his gums. He's spent months trying to be more mindful of little things, but on his way to the bedroom, he bumps into a bookcase, and he doesn't know whether it's his hand or his elbow that catches the belly of a champagne flute—a gift to Kerstin from Mutter —that he sends crashing to the floor.

"Is everything okay?" Kerstin calls out from her room.

"Yup," he says. "Nothing to worry about."

He stoops to pick up pieces and place them in the cup of his palm, drops shards of glass in a garbage can in the kitchen, then watches a black cat outside the window rub its back against a fence before it slinks near puddles, searching for a rat to carry off in its jaws. He's not about to draw attention to another of his fuck-ups. It only feeds a nervousness that burns in him like charcoal, white with heat, exposed to air currents that stoke, inflame.

He microwaves leftover mac and cheese in the kitchen for a minute and a half before he returns with a bowl to the bedroom.

Kerstin sits up naked on the bed, tapping away at laptop keys with her face lit up by swells of colour from the screen on her lap. While she writes, she listens to a CD of a gospel choir who sing with cracked voices, striving to loosen attachments to outcomes.

P.J. clambers on top of sheets beside her in paisley boxer shorts. "Hungry?" he asks.

"Nope," she replies.

"I've been craving carbs," he says. "Want some?"

"I'm good," she replies, intently studying the screen. "I'm writing Mutter an email. I have to confirm that I have the correct flight info. If I'm not at the airport on time to pick her up tomorrow, things will get ugly."

He drapes a calf over hers. "Are you looking forward to seeing her?" P.J. asks. "It's been two years."

"Not so much," Kerstin replies. "She's demanding."

P.J. waits for her to log off.

"I've got so much left to do this week." She tries to find a comfortable spot to lie in. "Out-of-town guests are starting to arrive and I'm behind on a draft of the article, so I'm going to have to work tonight."

"Work?" He places the empty bowl on the bedside table.

"I can't pursue the human-interest angle on the article anymore, but I did get a tip about industrial farming's involvement in the mistreatment of horses."

"Hmmm," he replies.

"You wanna look into it tonight?" she asks.

"It's after midnight."

"It'll make things less busy if I get it done now," she says.

"That seems...something better done in daylight."

"Come on, baby," she says.

"What about Schuld?"

"She's asleep."

"Checking an anonymous tip at this time sounds..."

Kerstin sits up again and picks at flaking polish on a fingernail. "I need to work." She gets out of bed. "If not, tomorrow will be a catastrophe."

"Take 'er easy."

She slides into a pair of jeans.

"Come back to bed, Kerstin. Everything will seem less urgent in the morning."

"I have stuff to do," she says.

He sits up. "I'll come with you."

"No, no." She feels reckless. "Keep an eye on Schuld. I got this."

P.J.'s confused. What's going on? It's unclear to him how he's the one who is being unreasonable. "What if something happens to you?"

"Make sure your phone is turned on." She kisses him on the forehead. "I'll be careful and call if there's a problem."

On her way out, Kerstin checks to see if Schuld's finally asleep.

* * *

2:49 a.m. Kerstin grips the chain-link fence surrounding the junkyard and clambers over the top, a video camera looped over her shoulder with a strap. Wire rips her jean pocket

155

when she leaps down onto gravel. Before her is a yard of rusty cars that line a dirt road that leads to a white portable at the end of the lot.

There's sludge in her from a lack of sleep that starts in her memory, knots in neck muscle, and mal-aligns painfully in her spinal cord. She passes a latticed boom crane that dangles a hook among untidy piles of flattened metal among hubcaps and coils of wire. Wind knocks around a loose-fitting sign above the door of the portable, and she can hear voices behind the building grow louder as she nears the front steps. Through a front window, flames dance against walls.

Kerstin gets down on her belly and drags herself over gravel using her elbows. Mashed glass scuffs her arms, petroleum fills her sinuses, and she slides between a hole in planks of wood attached to cement blocks that lift the portable off the ground. It stinks of rotten apples as she pulls herself through asbestos sheets and insulating pipes scattered throughout the crawl space. Then she wriggles toward another gap in the planks.

Illuminated by moonlight, three pregnant mares lie on top of plastic sheets. Two men in white aprons and surgical masks watch tubes inserted into the horses' stomachs extract blood into huge bottles already three-quarters full. The horses lie in their shit and blood. Eyes closed, their perforated bellies bleed out onto the sheet. Behind them, a stout man chain-smokes against a white Wozilla Pig Farms van. Kerstin manually focuses the camera lens on them through an opening in the lumber. It's sticky hot, and death sticks to her molars. She waits for one of the men to move, then takes her shot.

She feels a tickle at her calf, and as she turns, a black rat scurries away from her. Startled, she sits up, banging her head against the bottom of the floor.

"Did you hear that?" one of the men says.

"What?" the other replies.

"A noise under the building."

Kerstin holds her breath.

"Geezus," the second man replies. "This is a junkyard. Cats have a field day with all the fuckin' rats out here."

"I'm gonna take a look," the first man replies.

Kerstin slowly backs away until she's in the yard. Then she hot-steps it down the dirt road before she sprints toward the front gate. Feet slap against metal behind her, so she lunges for the chain-link fence. She grips the top rail, digs her feet between holes, and launches herself upward. When she drops onto the other side, the strap of the video camera catches on the rail. Fuckity-fuck! She watches in dismay as it snaps off her shoulder and falls down inside the fence.

"Over there," a man says.

Kerstin runs into a macadamia nut plantation and sprints through leafy branches that smack arms she uses to shield her face. Then she drops into a ball, waiting for footsteps to recede in the distance.

In sooty darkness, stinkbugs crawl inside her clothes and bite her skin.

8 Days to Wedding

<u>10:07 a.m.</u> "Rita Oozol didn't sign a new contract, so she's leaving *Switcher* at the end of the season," Kerstin says to Mrs. Ostheim at the airport's baggage check.

"That's just tabloid gossip," Mrs. Ostheim replies, her silver bangs immaculately styled with a curling iron and her floral dress neatly held in place by a matching sash at her waist. "She denies it."

"We were one of the magazines her agent contacted with an offer to do an interview with the announcement of her departure." Kerstin yawns. "It happens all the time."

Mrs. Ostheim falls silent and tries to remember what they're talking about through the splash of a migraine that bursts behind her right eye. "Rita is born again," she finally replies. "You've got to be incredibly cynical to doubt the sincerity of her denial."

"She's a businesswoman, Mutter," Kerstin sighs.

Mrs. Ostheim cringes. She doesn't like her daughter's overconfidence in her own opinions. Why does she have to be such an expert on everything when she knows so little about how to make her own life work? In fact, the reason

159

Mrs. Ostheim's flown in a few days early is to talk Kerstin out of making another life-changing mistake. Her fiancé is a drug addict she met online who's been sober for less than a year, she's known him for less than six months, and from what she can gather, he can barely support himself with the income he gets taking wedding photographs. However, if she doesn't time this conversation perfectly, the topic of their upcoming marriage will land her in an unproductive sludge.

"You look exhausted, *kleine Maus*,"[1] Mrs. Ostheim says. "Do they have you doing all-nighters at work right before your wedding?"

"*Nein*," Kerstin replies. "I just didn't sleep well last night."

"I know how busy you are with deadlines," Mrs. Ostheim says. "So I'll be fine keeping a low profile, and playing lots of Carcassonne with Phillip."

"It's Schuld, Mutter."

"Schuld, Phillip—I can't keep up."

"Schuld doesn't play board games anymore," Kerstin says. "She's a blogger now."

"*Oje*,"[2] Mrs. Ostheim says. "I hope she isn't illegally trying to access classified government documents."

Kerstin laughs. "She's a blogger, not a hacker, Mutter. She spends most of her time posting quotes on the internet from the books she likes to read."

"He'll—sorry, she'll—be busy as well then," Mrs. Ostheim says.

Kerstin keeps her eyes on bags that emerge from a tunnel on the conveyor belt. "I've cleared my schedule, and I plan to spend as much time with you as I can."

---

1. little mouse
2. Oh dear.

Mrs. Ostheim presses a finger against her temple for relief. "We could go horse riding together at the D-Lux Ranch."

"How about tomorrow afternoon?" Kerstin replies.

"That sounds wonderful, *mein Liebchen*."[1] Mrs. Ostheim is being agreeable to avoid pointing out the obvious: no matter what her daughter says, her life of perpetual chaos means she's rarely going to be around. The more some things change, the more others stay the same. Kerstin will end up working at the magazine right up until the day of the wedding. Therefore, she refuses to get her hopes up about an outing they had already put off during her last visit.

"There are your bags." Kerstin waits for two daisy-checkered suitcases to make their way toward them.

Once they're seated, Kerstin turns the key in the ignition of her Alfa Romeo, and the engine reluctantly turns over before it gasps to a stop. She leans back in her seat. "Don't quit on me now, Thurston," she says. Then she pumps the brakes before she turns the key. The engine sputters, and a plume of grey smoke spills out from under the hood.

"*Oh Gott!*"[2] Mrs. Ostheim says, grasping for the door handle.

"*Alles ist in Ordnung, Mutter!*[3] It happens all the time."

"Well, I'll wait outside while you figure it out, *Liebe*."[4]

While Kerstin pops the hood and takes a look, Mrs. Ostheim massages her temples and watches a silver-haired security guard in a neon-lime shirt observe them from a parking booth. It's embarrassing to have people see them like this. God knows she's offered her daughter money to

1. my darling
2. Oh God!
3. Everything is in order, Mother!
4. Dear

buy a better car a number of times, but there has been no interest in her help. Kerstin would much rather attach herself to damaged entities, much like she's doing with her photographer with a history of drug abuse. It's not the sort of example to set for Phillip, who has already chosen a life that embraces the destructiveness she tried to protect Kerstin from.

Kerstin opens the radiator cap, which hisses and sprays steam. She waits until the air clears before she fills the radiator with water from a bottle. Then she closes the hood and returns to the driver's seat to give Thurston's starter another shot.

Once they're out on the F-3, Kerstin weaves between small openings in a line of cars while driving thirty kilometres per hour over the speed limit.

"*Langsamer fahren!*[1] Kerstin!" she says. "I'd like to see my grandson once more before I die."

"She's your granddaughter, Mutter," Kerstin replies. "And don't fret so much. Thurston's great at beating rush-hour traffic."

Mrs. Ostheim grips the sides of her chair, unimpressed with Thurston's capacity to get from one place to another in a flash. Kerstin and she inhabit such different structures of time; she drops into it, peeling away each layer of the epidermis to get at an appreciation of the moment, and her daughter hurries through it to stay on top of being the protagonist in her life. How did it turn out like this?

"Can you at least turn on the air conditioner?" Mrs. Ostheim says. "The sun is coming through the windshield, and I feel like a boiling lobster."

---

1. Slow down!

"It doesn't work," Kerstin replies.

As she explains to her mother how to beat the heat by sitting at a 27-degree angle in her seat to maximize the airflow from the window, Mrs. Ostheim can't find the right words to say what she means—another side effect of Copax Ltd.'s blue gel cap despite its guarantee of seven hours of uninterrupted sleep. She struggles to locate the word bank in her brain, but is distracted by rising panic at being crammed in on all sides by neighbourhoods of houses packed together to accommodate the people who work in the plantations behind them.

"I don't suppose I should worry about the 'check engine light' on the dashboard," Mrs. Ostheim says.

"Absolutely not, Mutter," she says. "It's probably just a loose gas cap."

"Probably?"

"Most likely," Kerstin says. "It could be airflow pressure, but if that was the case the car would have shut down by now."

Mrs. Ostheim nervously giggles.

* * *

11:33 a.m. At the house, a shaky Mrs. Ostheim goes in to see Schuld, who lies in bed taking stock of how little she feels while stars get up again, and again like they will whether or not she's around to watch.

"Hey, Oma," Schuld says. "Long time no see."

"*Oh Mensch!*[1] Look at the state of you," Mrs. Ostheim replies. "Didn't I warn you the ocean has a life all its own?"

---

1. Oh, man!

"It musta really had it out for me then," Schuld says.

Mrs. Ostheim is shocked by the extent of the damage. It isn't so much that Schuld looks uncomfortable lying in bed with cuts all over her body and a bandage on her hand. It's more that her eyes are bloodshot from floating drowsily along on painkillers added to the meds to stop her from thinking too fast.

"*Kein Problem*,"[1] Mrs. Ostheim says. "Oma's going to take care of you."

"*Cool*," she replies.

Kerstin interrupts. "I hate to do this to you both," she says. "But something has come up at work, and I have to go out for a bit. I'll be back in a couple of hours."

Mrs. Ostheim isn't surprised. "Go," she says. "I'll make sure Schuld stays out of the liquor cabinet."

"Oma!" Schuld protests.

"I'm more worried about you than her," Kerstin says.

Kerstin slides on her sunglasses before she leaves her mother, who sits at her granddaughter's bedside.

* * *

11:58 a.m. Kerstin turns Thurston onto the F-3, a falsetto of tires braking in a web of intersecting highways. P.J. sits in the passenger seat, staring from his window, as they drive to see horses washed up on Ka'alipo Beach. In a tiny part of a universe contracting rapidly into a big crunch, they move forward into sunlight that is eight-and-a-half light minutes old. Sound is displaced by irrational numbers, pi, and soon

---

1. No worries.

they pass a prison surrounded on all sides by barbed wire and guards in turrets with immense Plexiglas windows.

"Are you angry?" she asks.

"No," he lies.

"I didn't have any service," she says. "Otherwise I'd have called you."

He looks down at his hands. They're trembling.

*　*　*

At the farthest point west on the beach, where the sand cliffs rise, P.J. and Kerstin wait behind a cordon of yellow caution tape. He adjusts his super-telephoto lens to isolate corpses being covered in white tarp by police officers before he takes a series of shots.

"How many bodies?" Kerstin asks.

"Two," he replies.

"Can I have a look?" He hands her the camera. "They're both pregnant, just like the ones I saw last night."

"This doesn't make sense."

"We need to look at Wozilla Pig Farms," she says. "And other pig farmers on the island."

"Why other ones?" he asks.

"There's a hormone, equine chorionic gonadotropin, that can only be found in the blood of mares in early pregnancy. eCG is used by some industrial farmers to boost the fertility of their pigs. So we need to find anyone who would benefit. Ranches. Farms. Companies." Kerstin hands the camera back to him. "Anything that fits."

"There was nothing at the junkyard when I tried to get photographs after you called this morning," he replies. "The owner died six months ago, and there's an eviction notice on the front door of his office. In fact, the only thing I saw was flattened cars and old tires."

A commotion erupts at the barrier, and a woman breaks through, sprinting toward the beach with caution tape tangled around the legs of her boots.

"Renomi!" she yells. "Renomi!"

A cop grabs on to her waist, pulls her down to the ground, and holds on tight as she screams.

"Calm down, ma'am!" he says.

She kicks and claws to get free while other uniforms pile on. They roll her onto her belly and hold her to the ground. Sand presses into her face.

"Do something!" Kerstin says to P.J. "They're hurting her."

He freezes, goosebumps on his forearms. "It's not our business," he says.

Kerstin starts to run toward the woman, and he chases after her, trying to remember what it was he learned at Narcotics Anonymous about how to be more assertive about his own point of view.

* * *

12:43 p.m. Gutya from the D-Lux Ranch sits on a log across from Kerstin. Her eyes are bloodshot and she twists a finger on hands coarsened by shifts from pelting rain to excoriating sun.

"I'm sorry for your loss, ma'am," Kerstin says.

"Oh God!" Gutya covers her mouth with a palm.

Kerstin hands her a tissue. "When did you see her last?"

"Last night," she gulps. "I stopped by the stables after six. She seemed fine. When I woke up, she was gone."

"Was there any sign of a forced entry?"

"No," she replies. "But the gate at the back of the ranch wasn't locked."

"It was open."

"No, unlocked." Gutya dabs at her tears. "It was locked before I went to bed. I check it. Always. Someone with a key must have done it." She looks at her hands. "Who would steal a pregnant horse? Who would do such a thing?"

* * *

<u>2:35 p.m.</u> P.J. takes in dollops of a memory of a memory as Kerstin sits across from him on the terrace of Café Dino's mid-afternoon, a cleft in the impressions that court him, meat space. They've spent the better part of their morning at the beach doing interviews and taking photographs. Now they take a break. He's been waiting for the right moment to talk to her about last night. He's upset that she took such a crazy risk going to the junkyard by herself in the middle of the night and disappointed that she takes pride in how she pulled it off. They really have no idea what they're meddling with. What if something bad had happened?

Pigeon droppings die on cement tabletops, their ashy craplets suspended in an air elongated by cloying humidity as she tilts forward in an orange dress. "One of the main reasons my marriage failed was because Tobias didn't want Schuld." She gently leans back in a plastic chair, then changes her mind and tilts forward again. "After she was born, I began to hear rumours that Tobias was screwing one of his clients. A model from an organic toothpaste commercial with an interest in broadcasting. And when I asked him about it, he accused *me* of an affair with Emmerich Voss."

"Ridiculous!" he exclaims. "You don't even like his films."

She slaps her brow.

"Sorry, go on."

She continues with a reference to an incident P.J. can't make sense of where Tobias spilled grape juice on her dress. (He doesn't know if he splashed it on her while she was in the dress, or if he went to her closet, took it out, placed it on a flat surface, and poured away.)

"You look terrific, by the way," P.J. says, after she has exhausted the topic.

She sighs. "*Danke*, baby." Then she checks her phone to see if there's a message from her father. Nothing still.

She really is a hop, skip, and jump in his abdomen, maybe his spleen (it's difficult to place). And while she talks about being in a good place for her mother's visit, P.J. notes a dimple on the outskirts of a pink, meaty pucker of a mouth.

"I'm trying not to smoke while Mutter is around to avoid having to explain myself." She folds one leg beneath her on the chair. "So I've spent most of the day munching on gum and sucking on nicotine mints." She pulls up a sleeve and shows him a patch on alabaster flesh plash with oils from the Dead Sea. "It makes me fucking edgy."

"I didn't catch the last word."

"On edge." She stares directly into his eyes.

"Oh."

"Quitting has made me edgy."

Kerstin leans forward to touch his forearm. And the mood changes, her mood, as she much too stingily defends a position—one she's attached to for now—taken in relation to her negative attitude toward Mutter. Then she checks again for lumps in lymph nodes and worries aloud about the return of a pain in the vicinity of her uterus.

"Mutter started obsessing about her health at my age," she

says. "She got herself a membership at the gym and began punishing her body so it would resemble a version of herself at twenty." She sits on both her hands. "And the thing is, she didn't even like being twenty."

As soon as Kerstin catches a glimpse of how she must sound, she employs a light touch, a rejoinder that keeps P.J. at a distance with a sharpness of tone that gets the conversation back onto her quest to get her arteries clear of nicotine. She stifles a yawn. Then is quick to locate an anecdote that is a further exhibition of poise—she talks about a recent dispute with a waiter over "a charge for trout when I ordered the salmon." Then she puts up a finger and answers her cell. "I have to take this."

She swivels away to whisper into the receiver.

On hanging up, she turns back toward him. "I gotta get back to the office," she announces.

P.J. flinches. He waited too long to bring up his feelings about her recklessness. "Is everything okay?" he asks.

"Eion likes your photographs and wants to use them with an article he'll post in four days."

"Wow!" P.J. replies. He apologizes for holding her up, and hates himself for it as she lifts her eyes to meet his, then quickly drops them like a dish of fluff, falling, flailing.

"I've got to get writing," she says.

"Go," he says. "It's been cool."

"Talk to Pop," she replies.

He's turns of mood as busy as fingers working the frets of an acoustic guitar.

* * *

After listening to Kerstin talk about quitting smoking, P.J. craves a cigarette, so he stops in at Duck-Huan's Grocery.

"Two packs or one?" Duck-Huan asks.

"One," he says. "No, sorry. Make that two."

"Two?"

"No, one," he says. "One is good."

In the background is a muted Korean soap opera on a twenty-inch television screen, and a bowl of noodles steams beside an open Bible sitting on a wide stool. P.J. nods toward the holy book. "Don't read the Song of Solomon."

"Why not?"

"It's smutty."

"Smutty?"

"Dirty. All about temptation. The language is sexual."

He smiles. "That doesn't sound like a bad thing to me."

"Can I ask you a personal question, Duck-Huan?" says P.J.

"Yes," he replies. "But not about sex."

"No, no," P.J. says. "It's about marriage. Do you tell your wife all your feelings?"

"Feelings change all the time, so I choose what to say carefully," Duck-Huan replies.

* * *

4:18 p.m. P.J. rides Aspen Towers' web-cammed elevator with Gee, the surf instructor from the second floor, who still fumes over his argument with the super in his office a few days back.

"Adrian's been threatening to kick me and my family into the streets," Gee says. "If he does, I'll tell the police about everything going on here." His unshaven cheeks are gaunt. "You see the envelopes the hookers push under his office door. This is money they give him to do business on my floor. Adrian doesn't think I know, but I know."

"When do you have to leave?" P.J. asks.

"Four days," Gee replies. "But I'm not going."

"You need a lawyer," P.J. says.

"I have no money."

The elevator opens on the fourth floor. "Legal aid is free, my friend. I'll get you their number."

"Okay," Gee replies.

P.J. holds the door with a hand. "One quick question," he says. "Do you tell your wife everything?"

"Like about the hookers?"

"Yes," P.J. says. "Well, not that exactly, but anything that you're going through."

Gee laughs. "Why make her worry?"

"Gotcha," P.J. replies before walking to 412, where he enters a spartanly furnished room with a tropical ceiling fan that whirs above linoleum tile. He discards his camera and keys by the door, loosens his belt, and collects himself by lying on the floor. Lubricated by an Americano, he prepares himself for a visit in the morning with Pop.

P.J. listens to fan blades merge with an upswing of sirens that clamour like a dull eruption of alarm clocks and recollects a grab bag of strip clubs, and balderdash, and the coke he's given up because of the entanglements it's driven him to. Is he in any position to judge his father for his drinking or for the sketchy way he's made his fortune? He's compromised by his own bad choices, and he hasn't had a problem benefiting from the plantation's profits when he needed.

More sirens purée the night.

A drizzle of bland hunger populates his belly, and he bottoms out, smoking a cigarette jacked between his lips.

Truth be told, P.J. gets along best with Pop when they keep it light. Television shows. Incoming cold fronts. Books they read. They don't even really talk when there are serious matters to deal with. Pop tells him how it's going to be, and he nods his head in agreement. Any departure from this ritual would mean relitigating their past, and the disappointing result will be an inability to give the experience a shared meaning.

P.J. drinks a fortifying guava juice, his eyes wide and wild while he staves off bad habits. His quest to transcend them drives him to work, or to get work, or to feel guilt about his failures with work (and it never ends). It makes him wish that time would jump forward several years, and he'd no longer be under the spell of a bad conscience.

How can he tell Kerstin what he's going through when he doesn't know if she'll marry him if she sees this chaos?

He can't sleep.

Windows clacks at joints, and outside, trade winds feel their way murmurously through palm trees, lollygagging toward a breach in the outer atmosphere.

7 Days to Wedding

6:17 p.m. In a purple sundown, Schuld and Woloff reassemble on the rolling green acreage of the Macmillan Cemetery before drinks with Precious and Eric: she draws in a sketch pad beside the mullioned windows of a building that survived a fire in 1903. Stone edifices regard them with disinterest as they listen to a mordant harp oozing from an apse. Among traces of smoke-darkened stone, they see a chapel's weather vane shiver in this bastion of crypts and engraved slabs, and winged seraphs blowing into trumpets, and stars of David and menorahs and sun crosses, and marigold flowers that are diseased and pining against ruins of pocked stone.

* * *

7:30 p.m. Woloff and Schuld walk toward Azar's Tavern. They squeeze their hands together while paprika-coloured horses drag carriages beside them, tapping their hooves against old cobblestone. Blank with sleeplessness, Woloff and Schuld make out a whirl of smudges, generalities. Logged out, adrift in unscheduled time. Separately and simultaneously, they move beneath a supermoon, high in the sky, its light gathered on the leaves of the foxtail palms.

* * *

7:45 p.m. They arrive early at a spot where on weeknights the beer on tap is three bucks, tea is served in samovars, and coffee is swilled from small porcelain cups in a room frequented by hookah smokers. They order ouzos with ice, make themselves comfortable at a table beside the air conditioner, and watch stragglers plonk down around them, eating orders of kebabs with rice that they wash down with pomegranate beer.

"This is going to be weird," Schuld says.

"Yup," Woloff replies. "The last time I saw Precious, she was fighting mercenaries. Now she's promoting a book."

"Does she know about me?" Schuld asks.

"Of course," Woloff replies.

"I mean, does she know I'm transgender?"

"Yes," he says. "That isn't something I hide from anyone."

Azar, the owner, checks in with customers at the next table. Over a soundtrack of lutes, he loudly pushes a theory about the existence of life on other planets transmitted by bacteria from satellites handled by human beings.

"Are you sure you aren't still a little bit in love with her?" Schuld asks.

Woloff reaches for her hand. "Of course, not," he says. "Why would you say such a thing?"

"It must be exciting to have a freedom fighter for a lover," she says. "Anything after that has to be a letdown."

"There's nothing remotely pleasurable about a life of con-

174

stant risk," Woloff replies. "All that does is make a person numb."

Beside them Azar talks about how he collects articles about earthlike conditions in outer space on the desktop of his iPad, then tells a story about communicating instantly with family members from great distances via a new app. Tables are loud with robust chatter about plans to use a long weekend to recalibrate chemistry that is out of whack, or to hold on to sanity by shopping among a happy circulation of goods. And behind them a couple talks of how tarp dwellers that line the median of the highway to outskirts are an eyesore.

Woloff stands. "There she is," he says.

Precious Namelok moves toward them in a lime dress that accentuates her high cheekbones. Behind her is a bespectacled man in a white T-shirt and faded blue jeans. Woloff and Precious briefly hug before introductions are made. Then they all arrange themselves around the table with couples sitting next to one another.

"*Hujambo,*"[1] Precious says.

"*Sijambo,*"[2] Woloff replies.

"*Ni vizuri kukuona tena,*[3] Woloff," Precious says.

"Yes, it is good," he replies.

"How long has it been?" she asks. "Three years?"

"Three and a half," he says. "It feels like a lifetime."

The recently engaged couple had a pleasant flight from the east coast, although it got bumpy with turbulence. Eric enjoyed the inflight movie and asks if it's true that the star, Rita Oozol, is from the Cove. There weren't any hiccups

1. How are you?
2. I am fine.
3. It's good to see you again

with customs, unexpectedly, nor with the taxi ride from the airport, and they're uncomfortable staying in the Glass Hotel, the glass building with penthouse suites on the top four floors that cost $6,000 per night.

"So you're an author now," Woloff says to Precious. "Much respect!"

Precious puts a hand on Eric's arm. "I couldn't have done it without him."

"She's being modest," he says. "I know people who read her manuscript, but all the work is hers."

They smile at each other.

"How's the running?" Eric asks.

Woloff looks down at the table. "I've had some problems with a wonky knee the last couple of seasons," he says.

"He's also being modest." Schuld holds Woloff's hand. "He made the 1,500 finals at NCAA last year. That's pretty good since he had only two months of training."

"You're a beast," Eric says. "You ran 3.26.56 at the Olympics as a freshman."

"3.26.86."

"That isn't standing around," he replies. "You'd have the gold if you hadn't faded at the finish, but who can blame you after you took it out so hard."

"That was a long time ago." Woloff looks over at Schuld. "Once I graduate this summer, I'm probably going to do something else."

Precious interrupts. "You're kidding."

"Nope," Woloff says.

"He's got options," Schuld offers.

"Like what?" Precious asks.

"I'm not sure," Woloff replies. "I like structure. Grad school. Stuff."

"Go back home, Rafiki," Precious says. "You're needed now the government has changed."

"Showing up *kama*,[1] 'Here I am, folks,' seems a bit..." Woloff replies. "I mean, you don't jump into a river to save a drowning man without a life vest."

"What about coaching?" Precious asks. "There's all kinds of running talent at home that would benefit from your experience."

"I've got my own shit to figure out," Woloff says.

Schuld squeezes his hand. "He's got it handled," she says.

"People change," Woloff says. "I've changed."

"No. No, I'm not judging," Precious replies. "But... Uncle Phineas is struggling to keep the garage open. He's your people. You don't get to abandon him because you've changed. That's not you, Woloff. You seem...lost. Look at all that makeup on your face, and you're quitting everything. Running. Your family. Building the nation's future. And no offence to Schuld, but making up a new identity is another out."

"What?" Schuld replies.

Woloff leans much too heavily against the edge of the table full of bowls, and it begins to rise from its hind legs. "That's not cool."

"I'm not making anything up," Schuld objects. "I'm a woman. I always have been."

"I'm a biological woman," Precious replies. "You just think you're one."

"You're a cisgendered woman," Schuld says. "That comes with many different experiences, but you can't accept mine as a woman as fully part of that."

---

1. like

177

"You have no idea what it's like to have children," Precious replies.

"Not all cisgendered women have children."

"This is ridiculous," Precious says. "When you talk, I hear someone who benefited from male privileges lecturing a woman about being a woman."

Woloff stabs a finger into the table. "You're being disrespectful."

Precious grimaces and cradles her belly. "Ouch!" she exclaims.

"Easy, baby!" Eric says.

"That was another cramp," she says to him.

"Sorry, folks." Eric stands up. "We're gonna have to cut this short."

Precious pats her womb. "I'm pregnant."

"Jesus and Mary Jones!" Woloff says. "You okay?"

"Just a moment." She takes several deep breaths with Eric holding her hand.

"Better?" Eric asks.

"Better," she replies.

"A baby," Woloff says. "Congratulations."

"Really?" she asks.

"Fersurely," Woloff replies.

She gets up slowly with Eric supporting her at her elbow, and they leave Woloff and Schuld to marinade in what's left in their wake.

After another ouzo, Woloff and Schuld walk over to the landing that looks out at barges in the harbour and huddle together under a yolky moon. Their insides feel scooped out, and all that is left is melancholy in their marrow. The sky sparks with dim stars, and they cannot see a future in the expanse of darkness that holds the night together.

6 Days to Wedding

<u>6:17 a.m.</u> Mrs. Ostheim's life is based on a principled engagement with the most mundane tasks. Therefore, on her first morning at Kerstin's place, she irons her dress for the day on a board set up in front of a gigantic ninety-inch television screen. Her mid-spine aches more than usual since she began to use the newly improved blue-gel sleeping cap, but the trade-off is that she fell asleep by nine-thirty yesterday evening. Now she's refreshed, so the vibrant colour on the TV makes for a more sharply focused version of life than she's used to. In fact, *This Week with Fred and Alice* has a much crisper version of her ex, Governor Ostheim, being a swell fellow ahead of the seven o'clock news.

Today, the governor talks about Freddy Kos, a man he met while visiting the homeless at a tent city at Denturra Beach Park.

"Freddy wants what we all want." He leans forward in his seat. "He wants a chance to live a productive life. He wants to be able to take care of his loved ones. He needs change." He looks into the studio audience. "I want to make a difference, and this is personal for me. I seek re-election in order

179

to continue work each day to give good folk like Freddy—people like many of you who've fallen on hard times—an opportunity to hold on to more of their paycheck. That's why I'm for the continual encouragement, through changes in regulations, of a more competitive macadamia nut market, an initiative that will bring an increase of 23 per cent employment to the island, and for the return of land on the east side to the Iqba Land Council, an endeavour that will lead to an increase of 17 per cent in land ownership by the local people. Unlike my opponent."

Mrs. Ostheim has heard it all before, but she admires his indefatigable talent for repeating himself with gusto as he makes the rounds during another election season. She's never been able to say the same thing twice without feeling like an imposter. It's too bad his talent for persuading others of his convictions never translated into his personal life. She recalls when Kerstin was still a child, she stopped believing in his speeches because his actions were seldom consistent with his words. Three-day-long weekends with the family were taken up with phone calls to donors, or else spent in marathon work sessions at the office. Even Christmas Days were taken over by matters related to winning news cycles and serving the interest of strangers needed for another run for office. Then, as a teenager, Kerstin began to mimic his way of talking for a laugh, and she soon found herself joining in because of how frustrated she was with dealing with her daughter's growing pains without him.

At the commercial break, Mrs. Ostheim goes to the kitchen to dig into groceries she bought to replenish her busy daughter's empty fridge. When she's made everyone omelettes, she sits on the patio with a cup of organic lavender flower tea and takes deep breaths while focused with withering intensity on the distant whirling blades of the tower mills on Mount Putnam.

Kerstin is the first to get up, ready for work in a white blouse and navy-blue skirt. She stands in the frame of the patio's sliding doors, her frosty hair tossed with gel.

"I don't have time for breakfast today," she says. "But not to worry, I'll get something in the café across the street from the office."

"I thought we were going horseback riding this afternoon," Mrs. Ostheim replies.

"*Tut mir leid, Mutter!*"[1] Kerstin says. "I'm on a deadline."

Mrs. Ostheim looks away. "I'll cancel our reservations then."

"Don't do that." Kerstin sounds irritated. "Treat yourself. Go. This trip is supposed to be fun for you."

Mrs. Ostheim's crestfallen, but she tries to remain upbeat as her daughter asks if there's anything she should bring home with her in the evening. Then she listens as Kerstin answers the question herself by going over all of the things she imagines an aged mother needs—a box of Kleenex, sticky pads for the floor of the shower, bath bombs.

"I'll bring back some sushi for supper." Kerstin kisses her mum's forehead. "P.J. will be joining us, so you can finally meet him."

Mrs. Ostheim takes note of how Kerstin has increasingly become demanding like her father. Her impatience leaks through in the ways Mrs. Ostheim feels rushed to agree to a shape to her day. Going horseback riding alone may or may not be how she wants to spend her afternoon, but talking about this will only worsen the chaos these visits bring

---

1. Sorry, Mother!

to the sense of order she maintains by living far from her daughter.

God forgive her.

The truth is, she's disappointed in Kerstin, who can't be bothered to spend any real time with her, so this trip has only disrupted whatever order she's been able to muster in her daughter's absence. Why does she expect anything different? When Tobias left Kerstin, Mrs. Ostheim found herself recruited to babysit while her daughter got an education. She spent hours keeping the boy entertained with board games, making meals, and going to his doctor appointments. She was there for Kerstin to depend on while her daughter struggled to pull herself out of a depression. Therefore, it seems selfish that Kerstin won't take an afternoon with the person who carried her for so many years.

"We haven't talked since I got here," she says. "I don't even know what you'll do when you move out of this place."

"We're fine, Mutter," Kerstin replies. "P.J.'s father has a beach house for us in Granger's Grove. It's near where I used to live when Schuld was born. I'll fill you in with details at supper."

"If you show up."

Kerstin is taken aback. "What's with you this morning?"

"You promise sushi for supper and sound concerned about my well-being, but I don't know if you mean any of it." Mrs. Ostheim's voice trembles. "There's always a deadline for this, or a meeting for that." Tears prick in her eyes. "I travelled a long way to be here, and you can't even make time for the breakfast I made for us to have together."

"I work," Kerstin replies.

"Yes, you're busy." She's sorry she can't keep her frustrations bottled up inside. "Go."

"You're ticking me off, Mutter," Kerstin says.

"*Du bist immer in Eile,*"[1] Mrs. Ostheim replies. "Have you even thought about why you're rushing to get married? You've known the young man less than six months. Six months! You met online. You have no idea who he really is."

"Is that why you came here?" Kerstin replies. "To tell me how messed up my choices are."

"He's a recovering drug addict without a steady career," Mrs. Ostheim says. "You can't count on the long-term stability of someone like that. This isn't the kind of mess you can easily get out of."

"I can't deal with your bullshit right now," Kerstin snaps.

"*My* bullshit!" Mrs. Ostheim says.

"Yes, your bullshit," Kerstin says. "You show up and hassle me about my fiancé." She grips hard to the door frame. "We're just fine."

"*Ach Quatsch!*[2] I raised Schuld when you were a baby with a baby," Mrs. Ostheim replies. "Me. That's who raised him. That's who took care of your bullshit then, and that's who is going to have to take care of it again when this all backfires on you."

"Why are you even here?" Kerstin says. "Is it to shit all over my happiness?"

"*Du machst einen Fehler,*"[3] Mrs. Ostheim says.

"Fuck you, Mum," Kerstin replies.

"Someone has to be honest with you."

"If you can't be happy for us, don't bother coming to the wedding," Kerstin says. "I really don't give a fuck."

---

1. You are always in a rush.
2. Oh baloney!
3. You are making a mistake.

As her daughter walks away, Mrs. Ostheim doesn't give a fuck either.

*　*　*

6:56 a.m. A sun-whupped morning creeps into the window above Schuld's head as she lies awake in bed next to Woloff while listening to Mutti and Oma argue. She itches under her Band-Aids, and when she rubs one spot, it triggers another that needs rubbing. While Woloff sleeps, she flips through a photo album with pictures of Urgroßvater and Urgroßmutter. She stops at a black-and-white shot, taken in the late 1930s, of a couple sitting on steps in front of a stone house, flowerpots on either side of them. A short dark-haired man wears an oversized charcoal suit and a bow tie, a cigarette hanging from his lips. Urgroßmutter is next to him in a blazer, a long skirt, and a cravat, her fair hair pinned back and parted left.

"What are you doing?" Woloff interrupts.

"Looking at pictures of my great-grandparents," she says.

"The ones who secretly lived as lovers?" he replies. "Can I see?"

"*Natürlich.*" She points to a wooden table in a village square. "For years they managed to conceal their love affair among cobblestone streets and bicycles and corner stores with window displays full of cans and bottles. A little before the war, Ernst Schröder, the brother of one of their good friends, became a low-ranking officer in the Nazi party. He was a handsome, clean-shaven paper pusher who wore a brown uniform with a *Reichsadler*[1] and the *Hakenkreuz*[2] on

1. imperial eagle
2. swastika

his chest. Ernst never fully accepted Urgroßmutter's rejection of his advances when they'd initially met, so he used his knowledge of her secret to blackmail and rape her."

"Jesus!"

"When she got pregnant with Oma, the couple decided they couldn't stay in Germany, and so they escaped a world that grew increasingly absurd to raise their child in East Africa."

Entangled in those parts of her past, Schuld wishes she understood more clearly, she wonders how the war changed them. What had they thought of the Jews, homosexuals, gypsies, and political opponents loaded into trains to be slaughtered in concentration camps? Had they known about the pregnant women and children sent to gas chambers? During those years, they were a couple that fled Hitler's Germany while one brother was sent to Russia to die in a camp and the other went to France at sixteen to serve as meat for the advancing Allies. What impact did this horrendous violence have on them? How much did it shape what they became?

"Whenever I look at these photos, I remember the war games I played with Dag-Christian, a childhood friend. We'd flip a coin to see who would get to be the tiny grey plastic German soldiers or the beige British ones. Afterwards, we set up our armies on opposite sides of the living room floor before dropping them with marbles rolled at them over carpets of territory."

"Do you have any photos of your great-grandparents in Africa?" Woloff asks.

"Oma grew up there on a farm with lots of uninhabited land, so they were freer and didn't have to hide in the same way." Schuld looks at another picture of a pride of lions that wandered out of the bush and onto their farmland, and she remembers their stories about puff adders, and talking waterfalls, and of the unDead that roam through *Licht*.[1] Then she points to a photograph of the couple in a Studebaker. "They owned that car when they lived there," she says. "Urgroßvater would drive Urgroßmutter everywhere because he said she looked so *'schön'* in it." She turns the page and shows Woloff cattle at a waterhole. "Their neighbour was a man named Matz Volker. Volker was married to the daughter of an earl who was a women's tennis champion, and my great-grandparents never liked him. He used to hunt on their land without permission, he wouldn't vouch for them at the country club, and on the day of the accident that left Urgroßmutter with a lifetime of migraines, he didn't warn them about the collapsed bridge on the main road." She closes the album. "It's one of the few things I've been told about them by Mutti, and I don't even know if she believes that's what really happened."

Woloff wraps an arm around Schuld's shoulders and drapes a leg over her waist, careful to avoid pressing against one of her wounded parts. "I'm gonna have to leave soon," he says. "I didn't sleep much because of the pain, so I gotta get another cortisone shot for my knee. Then I'm off to the courtyard to make some ducats selling Kush. But I'll hit you up again tonight."

"*Usiondoke*,"[2] Schuld says, pulling the sheet down to her waist.

"I have to go," he replies.

Humidity bubbles along Schuld's skin, and she's trapped by sweat that boils her outsides. "Stay." She doesn't want

---

1. light
2. Don't leave.

her day to play out the way it usually does. First things must be done first, and in the order they're always done. She'll eat breakfast because Oma has it ready for her. Then she'll go in for her work shift, sleepwalking through another day, more or less. "Meet my grandmother," she says, pulling Woloff onto her.

"Yesterday you said it was a bad idea," he says.

"I was being overcautious," she replies.

"Doesn't she hate black people?" Woloff asks.

"God, no!" Schuld says. "She grew up in Africa."

"There are lots of racist people who live there," he says. "Some leave to settle elsewhere and take their shit opinions with them."

"If anything, she dislikes strangers, so she might need a moment to warm up to you." Her fingers work the skin beneath his shirt. "*Ich liebe dich unendlich,*"[1] she says.

"*Ich liebe dich auch,*"[2] he replies.

He finds the jut of her hip as she reaches into the elastic of his underwear to explore a shock of his pubic hair.

* * *

9:13 a.m. Oma is reading a book on the couch when Schuld and Woloff enter the living room. She stands to shake his hand.

"It's good to meet you, Mrs. Ostheim," he says.

"Likewise," she replies.

He points to the copy of Günter Grass's *The Tin Drum* in her hand. "That's a fine novel."

---

1. I love you infinitely.
2. I love you too.

"Wolf is it?" she asks.

"Woloff," he replies. "O, ef, ef at the end."

"Natürlich," she says before turning to Schuld to say something else in German.

"Now?" Schuld asks.

"If you don't mind, Wolf, I'm going to have a quick word with Phillip on the patio," Mrs. Ostheim says.

After they disappear outside, Woloff picks up *The Tin Drum* and looks at the author's info on the back cover; but as he begins to read, the patio door slams and Schuld reappears out of breath.

"We're leaving," she says.

"Sure, bae," he replies, hobbling after her.

Schuld's neck is red, and she doesn't speak as she race-walks down the driveway.

"Wait up!" He stumbles through a pinching spasm in his hamstring. "I've only got one functioning leg."

She swivels around. "Shoot! I forgot."

"That couldn't have gone well," Woloff says.

Schuld pops a cigarette out of a pack of Marlboros and lights up.

"I didn't even get a chance to skim through Günter Grass's author info." He leans against a hedge.

"He lied about his Nazi past," she replies. "He's a dick."

"What happened back there?" Woloff asks.

"Can you give me a moment?" She flicks her cigarette onto the driveway.

They stand in silence.

"*Gummibärchen*,"[1] he says. "What's going on?"

Schuld tugs on a strand of her hair. "It's embarrassing."

---

1. Gummy bear.

He touches her forearm. "What?"

She bites her bottom lip to stop it from trembling. "She thinks I should have warned her that you were going to meet," she says. "She felt unprepared."

"For me being black?"

"Well, that isn't how she put it," Schuld says. "She doesn't want to pretend that I'm a woman and she worries that I'm messing up my life."

"That's fucked."

"She always acted like everything was fine," Schuld says. "But suddenly when she sees me in a relationship with someone, she's a different person."

"The world is full of judgmental people," Woloff replies. "Although you'd think her experience with her father would make her more sensitive."

"It's not what I expected from her," Schuld says.

The texture of the air stiffens around them, and distrust of surfaces made up of other people's words smother them like a burlap fog. Mrs. Ostheim. Precious. The Governor. Their stomachs crawl with puff adders. Anacondas curl in their intestines, their guts. So they pilfer a dime bag of his Purple Kush and bounce from right to west, listening to branches scrape against windowpanes, their frustration hot-knifed between the third and fourth ribs. As they sit on a park bench at Ka'alipo Beach, they churn like butter in a stippled urn, unable to see their way clear.

* * *

10:20 a.m. P.J. sits on a hardwood chair in the living room of his one-bedroom. He grinds his teeth and stares at a cork bulletin board. There isn't much to go on beyond grisly photographs of dead horses.

He's interrupted by a phone call from Kerstin. "Do you have a minute, baby?"

"Shoot," he replies.

"Can you hold on a sec?" Kerstin fields an inquiry about what to do with homophobic comments posted on an article by irate *Multi-modalZine* readers. "Eion is fine steering clear of the Sunderland family angle, but he says I don't have enough to make a link between the horses and the pigs. He thinks the statistical sample I'm working with is too small. There's a total population of over three thousand horses on the island and only six deaths. That's less than .5 per cent. I still think it's significant. He's not taking into account the fact that this has all taken place in the past couple of weeks. If six human corpses suddenly turned up with signs that there were connections, the FBI would be brought in. Am I right?"

"What exactly does he need?" he replies.

"Witnesses," she says. "But it's been tough for me to focus on tracking people down because I had an argument with Mutter earlier."

"What happened?"

She laughs. "She gets on my last nerve," she says. "I told her before she came that it was a busy week for me with the wedding, but it hasn't made a fucking difference. She still puts the pressure on me to spend time with her."

"You didn't lose your temper?"

"I did," she says. "I got so angry that I told her we already had the beach house."

"Oh!"

"Can you talk to Pop this afternoon?"

He hesitates. "I'm getting my tux. Remember?"

"Isn't he back at the office?"

"Sure," he replies.

"It's on the way," she says.

"But..."

"Please talk to him, P.J.," she says.

"I got it handled," he replies.

"Is that a yes?" she asks.

"Yes," he replies.

The truth is, he doesn't have it handled. He's flustered by the prospect of another task added to his schedule. He took the week off at the studio, but these last few days have been busier than planned. He still hasn't picked out his tuxedo and, unlike Kerstin, he has yet to coordinate matching garments with the grooms and best man. The reception at the Duncan Inn has been booked, but there's still a down payment to be made. He hasn't slept more than four hours the past couple of nights. Now he has to talk to Pop about the frickin' house. How's he supposed to do this? He and Pop have such different ways of making sense of the past—within the family, on the island they've grown wealthy on—and there's still tension over P.J.'s latest fuck-up that landed him in rehab. The latter is an area P.J.'s worked on. He isn't the undisciplined person he was before he went in a year ago, but Pop refuses to acknowledge how much he has changed. P.J. shows up at business meetings on time and has settled down with Kerstin. For crying out loud, he's even been planning to set up his own studio and to approach the police about hiring him to shoot crime-scene photographs. However, none of this is moving fast enough for Pop to continue to support him. He built his fortune by working long hours, living on a budget, and modernizing the way his company interfaced with global markets; therefore, P.J.'s relapse into drug use only confirmed his gut feeling that he's been too easy on his son by giving him handouts.

Morning sunlight fills his apartment. "Is supper still on with your mum?" P.J. asks Kerstin.

"At six-thirty," she replies.

After hanging up, he thinks of swings, and Labradors, and children running around in the backyard at Granger's Grove. Yes, he's only known her for six months, but she's good for him. She throws herself completely into whatever she's feeling, and that's something he wants to get better at. Sharing a life with her is the only reason he can come up with to stop himself from breaking his sobriety.

* * *

10:48 a.m. Another downpour soaks the Cove while P.J. munches on the last of a stack of leftover pancakes. Simultaneously, he goes over the list of personal effects to take on his rounds: his wristwatch, his keys, and his breath mints. Then he taps his back pocket, feeling for the envelope with a three-and-a-half-page letter for Pop to explain what he has learned he must atone for in Narcotics Anonymous.

A tropical ceiling fan whirs above him while cool trade winds course over linoleum tile, and rain glances from his gliding patio door that leads onto the balcony.

Done.

It no longer rains as he hurries down a short flight of stairs and toward orange construction signs on a slick sidewalk under repair. To his right is an empty lot bought in the seventies by a group from the Pacific Rim with plans to add apartment buildings to holdings in Ogweyo's Cove. Now it's clumps of riff-raffish grass and yellow election posters of Governor Ostheim and Colin Riverdale that hang from its fence of weather-beaten plywood. To P.J.'s left, To'o, a neighbour's child, is wrapped in diapers and lies on a straw mat in front of the building, where his parents leave him to air out on most afternoons. He's on his side, under an awning beside a parking lot with water that flows down its sloped surface. Raw data flashes past him at ground level; lime Crocs, socks worn with slippers, scarlet nail polish, flabby foot ankles that crush cockroaches among mourning doves.

P.J. tells himself to remain calm as he walks through the reverberation of a jackhammer that carves a square in the concrete. As he makes his way toward Pop's office, his skin tingles beneath a thin, sticky layer of sweat clinging to him like Vaseline. Up ahead, Duck-Huan carts boxes of sports drinks into his store on a trolley and doesn't smile while he disappears inside among an effluvia of diet pills, erection enhancement creams, shampoo that is the best the world has to offer, and egglike ivory balls that belch bubbles in the coloured water of lava lamps.

P.J. stops in for smokes. His last pack before he gives them up for his new life with Kerstin.

"Unpredictable weather," he says to Duck-Huan.

"But not so bad," Duck-Huan replies.

"Could be worse."

"Yes, much worse."

Then P.J.'s out the door with the letter he's revised multiple times in his back pocket, and he walks along Oslet Avenue, passing graffiti tags on park benches. He concentrates on long breaths. Handbills are taped to signposts that advertise the sale of goods belonging to another someone who has found it impossible to make a living in the Cove—

schemes posted on the internet have yielded only a smatter of supportive shout-outs from relatives. Nothing more. Farther along, there are shops and restaurants and bars that will be replaced by other shops and restaurants and bars, these transactions conducted by the recent influx of entrepreneurs who buy up the latest round of dirt-cheap goodies advertised on the posters taped to lampposts.

Tourists wrapped in towels have begun to stream into the onrush of sunlight, and into gift shops where they orbit around souvenirs. P.J. ambles past them, his face a placid mask as he tries to ignore a mind that flawlessly conducts negative speculations about how Pop will respond to their request to live in the beach house.

After leaving the main street, he pauses to stare at an upturned shopping cart, its wheels spinning and its metal glittering in drowsy light.

The last time he'd been bailed out by his father, he was mixed up with Sasha Bloo, the woman he met at the Sickle Moon, a club in the basement of the Glass Hotel, in a whole lotta lavish flutter. That night Sasha was all angles, hitting angular shapes in dry ice, her rump-rump shaking, her booty banging in neon limes. As strobe lights blinked, they bumped thighs for a couple of tracks before grinding against a mirror at the back end of the dance floor. Tempos doubled, trap beats flipped, and when they kissed, her pink wig tickled his forehead. At closing, they snorted coke and fucked in the back seat of her Corolla and on the hardwood floor of her one-bedroom, and then fell asleep after snorting and fucking again on top of a collection of glossy French *Vogue*s on her couch.

"Do we need to talk about this?" she asked afterwards.

"No." He slid into his jeans. "That was nice."

She lifted a finger and took as well as returned a text. "I dance at the Rialto Gentlemen's Club," she said. "Why don't you come by sometime and catch one of my sets?" Then she made another call and waved goodbye.

And so P.J. became a client, and a fan, who filled Sasha Bloo's garter belt with money he borrowed from his father. After he'd spent enough to pay down her car loan, they snorted lines of coke and made it again among boxes of liquor in a cluttered backroom.

She bit him, moved his hands to the places she wanted handled roughly, and asked him to pull her hair.

He didn't quite know what to make of it.

Sasha was not what she did for a living, he told himself. She was a businesswoman with a website, and a blog, and a webcam. She fielded offers to star in adult movies that went straight to DVD. Thus moved by her complexities, he announced that he loved her as they lay in her bed.

"You're cute," she said.

"I mean it."

"That's so sweet, hon," she replied.

And with that, she mocked frankness that should never have come out to play. She sent texts on her cell and perished against the kohl-dark outlay of the horizon.

For weeks, P.J. snorted Pop's money up his nose, wishing he could paint Sasha Bloo's toenails puce (even though this elixir would cost him gallstones). She will come around, he thought (and he knew this like he knew which tender spots in his gums had been eroded by stringy morsels of beef difficult to unstick from his teeth). For days, he followed her to strip clubs, and discovered she discarded new boots in a dumpster when newer ones come to the market. Then, on the morning she escaped to a quicker city that didn't know her many antics, he deposited himself in the mental ward of a wing built with a donation from his father, unable to locate himself by looking at spinning atlases.

* * *

10:57 a.m. P.J. gabs with Frankie Zhao, his dad's admin assistant, in the reception at the main branch of P.B. & Associates.

"How's Kerstin doing?" she asks.

"Busy," he replies. "She's balancing prep for the wedding with writing an article on the horses that have been dying on the island."

"Sounds busy," she says.

"Yup." P.J. points to the stacks of folders in front of her. "Do you need all those files even though you have computers?"

"You know your dad," she replies. "He likes hard copies of certain documents, so we shed originals and only keep these copies."

"He's lucky you put up with his eccentricities, Frankie," P.J. says. "He's even got you working on another Sunday."

"Only for a few more weeks," she replies. "This is my last month here."

"Whut?"

She leans over folders and begins to whisper. "I've been asked to take a pay cut, and quite honestly, I can't afford it."

"A pay cut?"

"You know your father." Her elbow knocks a box of labels to the floor. "He's worried about the tariffs getting lifted, and so a lot of people are either losing their jobs or taking salary cuts."

"But you've been with him for over fifteen years."

She disappears beneath the desk before reappearing with stack of labels. "Loyalty doesn't mean what it used to with the company."

"You deserve a pay *raise*," P.J. says.

"You'd think so," she replies.

"I'm sorry," he says.

She labels another file. "I am too, P.J.," she says. "I thought we had a different kind of relationship than we actually have."

* * *

11:00 a.m. In his father's office, P.J.'s brain lurches with light particles that survived a trek from the sun's core. What does he need to remember? He's in a good place now, he's a better person than he was a year ago, and he has learned that he must take it day by day.

However, once in Pop's domain, all the work he's done on himself starts to unravel. He forgets about the letter in his back pocket, and hair follicles on his neck stand on end as he sits across from his father, who presides imperiously in a charcoal suit behind a desk, his Rottweiler, Gixx, lying on the floor beside him.

"The governor just called to wish me a happy recovery." Pop snorts derisively. "Great guy, huh! I'm back at work, for Chrissakes. I'm already recovered."

"He's been good to me." P.J. had met him briefly at a fundraising dinner he'd gone to as Kerstin's plus-one. "Really welcoming."

"Well, he was pretty uncivil to me," Pop replies. "He's not open to a discussion about his stance on the land and now he's making noise about additional tariffs."

"It's personal for him," P.J. says. "It's the main issue he's running on."

"Bullshit." Pop pushes around a paper clip on his desk with a finger. "He's looking at algorithms collected from polling data and focus groups. This is a calculated political gamble."

"He's not like that," P.J. replies. "Maybe if you spent more time with him you'd see this."

"You've always been gullible, Junior," Pop says. "The man has only survived in the game because of his political instincts. Except in this instance he's wrong. We live in an oligarchy that thrives on protectionism, and the cost of doing business will mean he'll lose the election."

P.J. pinches skin above his wrist to keep calm. "Well, I like him."

"You ought to rethink how quickly you're rushing to become part of that family," Pop says. "One thing I've learned over the years is that the apple doesn't fall far from the tree."

"Kerstin is her own person," P.J. says. "Whatever you think of her father and his politics, it has nothing to do with her."

"Listen, Junior." Pop crumples a sheet of paper before hurling it over his son's head at a trash can near the door. He misses. "You've made some great strides since you stopped doing coke, but I hate to see you make decisions that put you back in that situation again. You're going to be a father to her transvestite daughter, but you're still figuring out how to take care of yourself."

"It's transgender," he says.

"You know what I mean."

"We're getting married next week, Pop." P.J. digs a knuckle into his thigh to keep from snapping. "Get used to the idea because it's happening."

"The deal isn't done until you say, 'I do.'" Gixx breaks his down-stay, and Pop digs a knee into his dog's ribs. "Down!"

The animal snarls.

Pop slaps the dog hard on the snout with an open palm. "Down!"

"Jesus!" P.J. says.

"Down!" Pop smacks him again. "Down!"

Gixx relents, lying back at his feet.

"I came here to ask for your help." P.J.'s hands tremble as he explains how he's getting back on track and how Kerstin has played an important part in his recovery. Then he talks about love and commitment and growing up and so on. After he has established the irrefutable premise that the two of them belong together, he lays out his proposal. They'd like to rent the vacant beach house after the wedding at a reduced rate. When he goes over a projected budget, his father walks to the office door, drops the ball of paper into the garbage can, and returns to his seat to tug at a rubber band on his wrist. "This is a positive step for us, but we need your help getting on our feet, Pop. It'll only be a short while before I'm making a steady income at the studio. Meanwhile, people at the magazine are really happy with Kerstin's work. She's their top candidate to fill a senior editor vacancy that'll happen within the year." He scrunches his hands into fists to steady them. "If you help us out, we'll increase the amount of rent as we get more financially stable."

"I wish you weren't always on your way somewhere," Pop replies. "For the love of God, you're forty-three years old, and I've been keeping you afloat financially for years." He clears his throat. "I tried to warn you about choosing a career as a photographer. You're broke most of the time and you rely on money from me to get by, something I doubt you've shared with your bride-to-be. Even if you do by some miracle get your studio up and running, you still won't come close to making what you'd get in an entry-level management position with my company. This is hardly a way to enter into a marriage, let alone take on one with a woman who already has a transvestite child."

"So you won't help us."

"This is a consequence of your choices." Pop removes the rubber band from his wrist before he flicks it over his son's head toward the garbage can. "If you want to move into the beach house, you need to come to me with a business plan and not a wish list."

"Please don't do that," P.J. replies.

"What?"

"Can't you do something because it's the decent thing to do?" P.J. is jittery. "Not wrangle for the best deal. It's so... imperialist."

"You mean white," he replies. "I hate to point out the obvious, but you're white too."

"I'm half, Pop," P.J. says.

"Half. Full. Look, you get one shot at life, and here you are acting like a clown," P.J. Sr. replies. "Think this through better. Don't use the past to rationalize your failures in the present and don't paddle against the tide by getting married."

P.J. stands abruptly. "We'll manage on our own."

"I'm only looking out for you, Junior."

"You're a hypocrite." P.J. unloads with a number of examples of his father's drunken womanizing over the years, and talks about how much that hurt both Mama and him. "Don't you feel any guilt?"

"Regrets are for the weak," Pop replies.

On his way out the door, P.J. kicks over the trash can. Then he passes Frankie, who fields calls on a headset while she fills a cup at a water cooler. She winks at him. He waves back. Then he legs it to a hallway lined with inspirational quotes by Captains of Industry on large canvases.

After he's had a moment to collect himself, he phones Kerstin. "Good news! Pop came through for us." He's too ashamed to tell her how stingy P.J. Sr. can be. "The house is available in a month. Pop will give us the place for $1,200 a month for two years. Great, huh?" He'll come up with a way to spin this after the wedding. "He wanted us to move in with no charge, but I thought it was important to pay to show that we're not taking advantage of his generosity."

"That's absofuckinglutely fantastic," she replies.

"I told you things would work out," he says.

"When can we go see it?"

"After the honeymoon," he says. "There's some business-client guests who'll be moving in in three weeks, but we can always drive by to take a look."

"You just made my day," she replies. "I love you so much, baby."

"I love you too," he says. "I'll see you at six-thirty for dinner with your mum." After he hangs up, he stares out a window, craving a bump of molly.

* * *

1:09 p.m. Before the elevator closes on the ground floor at Aspen Towers that afternoon, Mrs. Wainwright from 608 calls out for P.J. to hold the door.

"Yoo-hooo," she singsongs.

She has drawn her eyebrows on with an eye pencil, and she wears another in her collection of green cotton dresses.

"I'd like you to take a look at this." She clicks away at her Blackberry and calls up a recent photograph of an empty packing box beside his door. "This is not how we maintain the hallways in the building." As the elevator rises, she clicks onto additional shots she's taken from a variety of angles. "I know you are leaving us soon, but some of us still have to live here."

"The lighting isn't the best in the first one," P.J. responds.

"Are you being a smart mouth?" Mrs. Wainwright asks.

"Next time use the flash," P.J. says. "It'll get rid of much of the graininess."

"Hmmmpfh," she says as he gets off at the third floor.

P.J. escapes into his hallway, goes into his apartment, and locks the world out while he rummages through a cupboard for a camomile tea. He just has to wait. Things somehow work themselves out. If he keeps his mind on the success of his desired outcome, the universe will present a way out of his dilemma.

* * *

2:05 p.m. Horses are tied to poles in an enclosure where they flick their tails at flies that land on their haunches. Nearby, Mrs. Ostheim stands on a box and waits while Gutya, the owner of D-Lux Ranch, leads Culvert, a grey mare, beside her.

"Are you ready to rock 'n' roll?" Gutya asks.

"Yes," Mrs. Ostheim replies with more force than conviction.

She puts her foot into a stirrup and climbs onto Culvert. Once adjusted in the saddle, she's handed the reins.

"Awesome!" Gutya says. "You're good to go."

Mrs. Ostheim squeezes her knees into the mare's sides. Then Culvert ambles forward to join a mother and her daughter who linger on their horses outside a front gate, wearing wide-rim hats. The humidity makes it difficult for her to get comfortable in skin sticking to her clothes. She's still upset about her confrontations with Kerstin and Schuld. Someone has to be willing to tell the truth. Something has to be done to keep them from making such disastrous decisions.

When Mrs. Ostheim reaches the others in the riding party, she meets Tola, who brought Odon, her eight-year-old daughter, as her plus-one. They wear matching white jodhpurs, scarlet sweaters with patches on their elbows, and black knee-high boots. Both have lots of experience riding in Wyoming, where they live, but they're using the afternoon to ride on a beach for the first time.

"It's a hot one," Mrs. Ostheim says.

"Ninety degrees," Tola replies, dabbing at sweat under the visor of her helmet with a handkerchief.

"It's ninety-one," Odon says.

"It feels hotter without a breeze," Mrs. Ostheim replies.

"Let's do this," Gutya says, joining them.

They follow her onto a narrow path that runs through a field overgrown with weeds. At the rear, Mrs. Ostheim firmly holds on to Culvert's reins as she breaks into a canter to keep up with the others. She bounces in place on her saddle, watching Tola with Odon in their identical outfits. She thinks about all the time she spent on activities with Kerstin wearing the clothes she'd picked out for her. There were trips to zoos and museums, attendance at the theatre and symphonies, hikes into trails on Mount Putnam, and all of those days at various beaches in Ogweyo's Cove. What did it all add up to? *Eine Katastrophe.*[1] She's divorced from the governor, alienated from her child, hated by her grandchild, and riding alone at the D-Lux Ranch.

Up ahead, Odon's horse halts abruptly, so Mrs. Ostheim yanks hard on Culvert's reins to stop the horse from bumping into them.

"Help, Mum!" Odon says as her horse turns his head to chew on weeds beside the path.

"I got this!" Gutya announces.

She rides over to Odon, grabs her reins, and gives them a tug. The horse poops, but doesn't budge. While Gutya struggles with the animal, Mrs. Ostheim thinks of how big a mistake it was to come on this trip. Her daughter has a mind of her own, and all Mrs. Ostheim manages to do is get in the way with suggestions that don't fit the plan. There's only Kerstin's way, and any deviation from the map in her daughter's head is wrong. It takes a hard line to get her to act responsibly. *Wie nervig.*[2] She doesn't need the hassle.

Gutya drags the reluctant horse forward, and Mrs. Ostheim flicks Culvert's reins and relaxes in her saddle. As the group descends toward Ka'alipo Beach, she can feel the horse's attunement to the slightest change in the position of her hands. The trail twists through a promontory of rocks before they enter an open bay.

"Good job, everyone." Gutya leads them into shallow water that laps around the horses' hooves.

Mrs. Ostheim stares at waves cresting in pale-blue water, outside the experience she wants to be having. She's inside

---

1. A catastrophe.
2. How annoying.

reasons not to go to Kerstin's wedding. *Es ist eine Farce,*[1] and she doesn't see the point in pretending any different. In any case, why make the effort? *Wozu?*[2] Have they ever even been close? Raising Kerstin was seldom a joy. She screamed instead of talked, and it made it difficult to listen to her for any length of time. She even taunted the neighbour's retriever by setting off firecrackers, and eventually, the stress gave her an ulcer. What has changed? Nothing. Kerstin's building a life with a man without a job and a taste for cocaine. Her grandson needs to be in counselling for his deviancy. Their lives are insane, and any constructive suggestions make Kerstin angry. How can she care for a person who rejects anything she has to say because it comes from her? It reminds her of Urgroßvater's *and* Urgroßmutter's selfishness in insisting on being a normal family, of the isolation she felt because of it, and of her disappointment at growing up in a foreign place without a real father.

* * *

6:10 p.m. In the living room that evening, Kerstin folds laundry, fuck. She tried to make peace with Mutter by apologizing. They argued about P.J. again. Mutter threatened to go stay at the Glass Hotel. Kerstin didn't object, adding they have free weights. Mutter left in an Uber, but her departure hasn't helped to rid her of anxiety that looms behind her right ear. She can't tell P.J. what her mother thinks of him, and she's submerged in futility as to what it means to have meaningful encounters with other people. Relationships

---

1. It's a farce
2. For what?

make her feel used and thanked and abused and apologized to and then discarded at the end of it all. Is it possible to avoid getting reduced to what others expect of her? How is she supposed to coexist with these people? Yes, P.J. isn't Tobias. He listened to her and came through with the beach house. However, she can't shake the feeling that Mutter is right about his lack of stability, and that he's probably one fun moment with a stranger away from giving himself to a less difficult person.

She adds Schuld's T-shirts to a teetering pile of her clothes, tries another call to Papi, and then, to keep from raiding the fridge for waffles smothered in maple syrup, she begins to pair off Schuld's socks.

She's got her own to work do. There have been rumours of mares being used for eCG, but more like the odd unattributed story online. To make the case that it's an unacknowledged industry practice, she'll need to find more farms and companies she can build her evidence around. Unfortunately, she can't get herself started making calls. Instead, she thinks in uncontrollable ways about whether she's where she ought to be in relation to where she is. Forty-two and she still shies away from the ways she responds to her encounters with bodies in the world—the ones that make her careful in their presence with all the brutality they carry, the ones that make her worry, the ones that excite her with sensations that make her question the adult choices she's trying to make, the ones like P.J.'s that she doesn't know if she can trust, and the ones like her mother's whose judgments throw her into doubt.

Nothing survives the clanging stars, she murmurs to herself, and feels worse (every day is worse and worse, even though there is much in a day that makes it better).

* * *

<u>7:07 p.m.</u> Since dinner with Mrs. Ostheim was cancelled, Kerstin and P.J. decide to make the most of it by celebrating the good news about the beach house. Therefore, they sit in plush crimson seats at the Palace Movie Theater and wait for the beginning of *Quack*, director Emmerich Voss's latest vehicle for his muse, Rita Oozol.

"Navajo hipster panties are ridiculous," Kerstin says about a window display they saw in a store next door. "They're the absolute worst kind of cultural appropriation."

"Everyone borrows from somewhere," P.J. says. "What isn't appropriated?" He isn't sure why he's being so contrary. "The Egyptians and Mesopotamians borrowed from each other. The Greeks from the Egyptians. We're all products of what came before. There's no pure culture." He knows there's more to it. There's the appropriation of the land by settlers, something he knows well since his grandfather bought up farmers' land leases to start what became P.B. & Associates. He benefits from all this appropriation, and he builds his life on the foundations Mama's people were uprooted to secure. "Anyway, there's something troubling to me about the idea of a pure culture. It's one step removed from eugenics."

She's stunned. "What benefit was it to the Egyptians to have influenced the Greeks? Very few people remember Plato studied in Kemet? Instead everyone goes around thinking Europeans invented civilization. *Mein Gott.* You think the Navajo get anything in return from the sale of panties? Nope, they get bubkes for the use of their name." She reaches into the popcorn. "And did you really mean to compare a community's desire to protect their culture to eugenics?"

"Forget I mentioned buying a pair of Navajo panties." P.J. lowers his eyes. "I thought they'd add spice to our honeymoon."

"Why not buy me a Native headdress to wear while you're at it?" Kerstin's voice shakes. "Who cares if it's sacred? Anything goes if there's a market for it."

"Fuck, Kerstin!" he replies.

"Don't talk to me that way," she says.

They get quiet for several minutes. Unhappy. Sullen.

P.J. puts a hand on her leg. "I'm sorry," he says. "There's so much going on right now." He gently squeezes. "It'll be fine. Everything is taking care of itself."

Kerstin takes a series of quick breaths. It isn't fine. She can't be honest with him like they promised one another. Why? P.J. thinks so differently than her. They're supposed to be teammates, but they're rarely on the same page. It was so difficult getting him to act on the beach house. She tried to overlook his lack of objection to the rough treatment of Gutya by the cops, and this latest tone deafness to the experience of the Navajo isn't working for her.

As the trailers begin to show upcoming features, she digs into popcorn and stares hard at the screen.

The movie is a psychological thriller about Itz Unger (Matthias Müller), a lion tamer at the circus, and his lover, Tanisha Brixton (Belinda Salisbury), a tightrope walker. The early part of the film focuses on the lovers as they tempt death while doing exploits of increasing risk for high-class clientele who bet on which of them will be first to meet an untimely end. Itz has the first big scare when flashbulbs blind a lion sitting on a footstool while he circles around it with a whip. Confused, the cat lashes out, mauling his shoulder before the creature is shot. While Itz recovers in hospital, the couple seeks counselling for the anxiety their respective passions cause each other. They meet Dr. Kaplan, played by Rita Oozol, and she has a secret that causes her to sit on park benches being sad. From that point on, it's a series of visits to the shrink, and questions about whether Dr. Kaplan is a quack; however, their need to return for definitive answers to their dilemma eventually forces an honest confrontation with the psychiatrist. It's revealed that Dr. Kaplan is a proxy for the film director, and the characters are actors in a production of a film about a lion tamer and a tightrope walker. Then the movie ends happily with a wedding that incorporates the fully assembled cast and crew breakdancing down the aisle of a church.

Afterwards, Kerstin and P.J. stroll into the lobby, out past popping corn and into the street in front of the window display of a mannequin wearing Navajo hipster panties.

"That wasn't bad," P.J. says.

Kerstin couldn't disagree more. She glances at a bulletin board covered in posters of her father trading on his name for the power it gives him to be busily beyond reach. He's a mask of foundation and blush that reveals, instead of hides, the signs of age they're meant to distract from. "That twist at the end," she replies. "I could see it coming."

"Really?" P.J. says, thinking of Pop's gift for predicting storylines, and of how he's predicted his marriage will end in divorce.

* * *

10:34 p.m. Back at the apartment, P.J. and Kerstin lie on a bed with lit candles on side tables. Sticks of patchouli incense burn on a dresser, and an iPod plays a selection of house ballads downwind from the window. Outsides disrupt their insides. There's touching, and lots of it everywhere. Fingers travel over skin, cup nipples, and tongues loll along the outline of ribs.

"Stop," Kerstin says.

"What?"

"I can't do this," she says.

"Is something wrong?" he asks.

"I just feel...upset."

He slides a hand over her waist. "It's going to be okay," he says, wondering whether things will really be okay this time.

Outside, cars pull in and out of spots as Kerstin thinks about how they should be spending this time before their wedding on unbridled fucking, as the general public agrees is expected. Instead, she lies awake imagining the meanest things about her husband-to-be with a coke habit. Marriage isn't their only choice, unlike for their parents. She hates the utter desperation that seemed to lie at the heart of that relationship, a pathetic need to share a life with someone, no matter how ill-fitting that someone else might be. How are her choices any different from theirs? Once she strips away all the romantic stuff, that sugar-coating, maybe she just does better when she's not alone. It's easier to sort out all the pragmatic everyday survival things together with P.J., rather than by herself. Is that so awful? Is it? She focuses on breathing, in through her mouth and out through her nostrils. What does she really want from P.J.? She wants to be so in love with him that she laughs and laughs and then cries because she doesn't know what else to do with all that happiness inside her. And she wants their moments together to outshine the trivialities and irritations of everyday life, and not the other way around.

5 Days to Wedding

<u>10:48 a.m.</u> At Woloff's place, Schuld leans back on sofa cushions with her legs open, wearing white lace undies, a pair of stilettoes, and an anklet with a pair of silver bells. Her mouth is gashed deep red with lipstick, her bushy hair falls down over her eyes. One hand cusps around her tit. She licks her other hand, turns to face the wall, and then she reaches between her thighs and tugs on her penis.

Behind her, the frame of a painting bumps against the wall.

Schuld backs up Woloff's ventricles, and puddles in his chambers... Jesus and Mary Jones, babe, he's a klutzy boy carrying around impressions of her like water carted from the river to the village, *and* he's full of an irresponsible wish to buy her a necklace that would dangle from her neck, flashing with the light of the new moon...pearls, sulphur.

Drifting asleep then awake, Woloff finds Schuld reading Dietrich Bonhoeffer's *Letters and Papers from Prison* and smoking a spliff in his bathtub.

He sits on the edge of the basin. "What do you see yourself doing in five years?" he asks her.

"Is that a serious question?"

"Uh-huh."

"I'ma be a world-class pole vaulter," she says. "What about you?"

"I'ma be a top-notch jockey," he says.

"Aren't you too big for that?" she asks.

"Not if I'ma be an anorexic," he replies.

"I'm really asking," she says. "Where do you see yourself in five years?"

He dips a hand into the sudsy soup of tepid water and splashes it into Schuld's tangled hair, teasing apart knots while he kneads her skull with his fingertips. "Sometimes it feels like I belong to a world that doesn't exist yet." He touches her neck, her flesh warm like fresh bread. "One made of scattered parts from everywhere." They get silent again, taking in stories they're trying out as ways to accurately describe themselves before they switch positions in the tub. "In five years...I want to be in that world."

She lathers his back before splashing it with water. "*Küss mich,*"[1] she says.

He turns, kissing her pink swell of lips. Excitement arises in him like dough. It feels like a bottomless reservoir of more of him fitting with her. *Ich und du.*[2]

"I love you," he says.

"I love you too," she replies.

His hand encircles her hardened cock as she pinches his nipple, fluorescent lights flickering above them like clownfish circumrotating coral.

---

1. Kiss me.
2. I and thou.

* * *

<u>1:42 p.m.</u> Schuld sits with Woloff on a terrace that looks out onto a stone courtyard in front of the Glass Hotel. A fountain spouts water at its centre from the mouth of a mermaid. Visitors to Ogweyo's Cove lean over tables to swill from pitchers of brew. Their accents boot with cosmopolitan swagger, cigarette smoke crawls from their ashtrays, and, for a microsecond, Schuld thinks of the future they planned that morning. They'll wake up every day with a mission to do one task each day toward their eventual move to a house with a garden on the wilder west side of the island—she has room on her credit cards if they need it; all she has to do is make sure she holds back on her natural impulse to splurge on art supplies. If he's going to stay in the country, he has applications to make to graduate school and a visa to sort out. Details for another time. To celebrate, they're going to the Sickle Moon tomorrow night for the first time since Schuld was assaulted.

Off-kilter in the new, their thoughts bump against gangrenous sunlight. "Is the calm life worth living?" Woloff asks. "You know, is it possible to find meaning in life without creating an adrenaline-induced sense of drama?"

"Shit, bae," Schuld replies. "I don't think people would get out of bed without the drama."

In the courtyard, those who got out of bed line up at booths to buy trinkets, hats with wide brims, and postcards. Others stand in front of cameras in groups of three or four, wearing their favourite looks. They smile to show laser-brushed gums before angling their heads.

"Hey, Woloff," says a tall dude with a purple birthmark on his arm.

213

"Luke, my man," he replies.

They shake hands, trading weed for cash hidden in their palms.

"If you hear of a reasonably priced apartment—"

"House," Schuld interrupts.

"—house on the west side, can you let me know?"

"No doubt," Luke replies.

Vacationers descend in ravenous packs on designated photographers to examine recently shot pics. Positive. Optimistic. Behind them, bromances bloom as men in shorts scowl into lenses, their arms crossed in front of them.

A woman in a visor stops by their table. "What kind today?" she asks Woloff.

"Kush," he replies. "It's choice."

"A quarter?"

They make an exchange with a handshake. "You're gonna love these buds, Linda," Woloff says.

"Thanks, Woloff," she says.

He asks her to keep an eye out for house rentals on the west side, and she winks, promising to look into it.

Sun straddles the sky, tilting as it drags its burning rump through the day.

Woloff looks at his watch. "Oh, shit. I've gotta pick up my motorbike from the garage before the place closes."

"Finally."

"Yup, they've had it over a week."

While Woloff pays for their chai teas, Schuld picks up her skateboard, and soon they walk out into a run of store windows with antiques, ottomans, and rugs. On their outskirts, among forty-storey high-rises and three-thousand-room hotels, people stand in packs that scooch down before digital cameras on selfie sticks effervescent after a fresh night's rest.

"You good?" Woloff asks.

"Uh-huh," she says. "You?"

"Never better," he replies.

When they kiss, sleeplessness pilfers Schuld's ability to understand why she's alive (and why now).

* * *

4:53 p.m. A stiff breeze blows up a median on Logan Street, heaped with tilting tarp and hermits who wage battles with vermin. Next to them, gusts of wind swivel in brakes of cars stacked impatiently behind one another.

Schuld skateboards into fat sun slung low on the horizon. Cuts chafe at fresh scabs beneath her clothes, the dog bite in her shoulder aches, and pain pulsates in her hand.

It makes sense for her to be on her own again. It's a good time to make changes. She doesn't believe in a deus ex machina, or a God named fortune, but she does in the moments Woloff slides next to her beneath the covers of the bed.

The taste of boiled eggs is swinish in her mouth as she rattles along a walkway the length of the park's greenery. She pops a stick of spearmint between her teeth. Squadrons of flying ants swoop around her, then scatter into formations that quickly disappear into eucalyptus trees. Wind kicks up, and she grabs for the brim of a baseball cap pulled down around her ears.

Too slow, and off it blows toward Logan Street, where it disappears beneath the chassis of a Honda Accord.

Fuck it!

She's careful to avoid Dr. Salao, in a green polo shirt, riding toward her on a bicycle that is too small for him. He wobbles,

215

knees wide, while beside them, in open parkland, kids play soccer, making pretty passes with their heels, dribbling at a full sprint while surveying the field around them. Then they settle on chances from forty metres out.

Schuld thinks of the night she moved in with Mutti on leaving the hospital with her broken arm. She sat alone on the terrace in a cast, and she cried, thinking of a skinny bird covered in tar she once found in the park—she took it home, fed it electrolytes with a syringe, and cleaned off its wings with vegetable oil. Then she wrapped it in a towel on her lap, and she talked to the bird and she wept, and the bird was so calm, it just looked at her and bled from its beak, and then it died.

A soccer ball rolls in front of her. She kicks it back before skating through a gate and under sneakers hung by laces from telephone wires. She emerges on the edge of a highway that curls like scattered strands of spaghetti around itself. Then she coasts on the outer edge of churning traffic, turns left at Dongwai Street, and rapidly glides by people who live behind pine hedges that line Woodsword's Estates.

She's nervous about returning to the club, but it was her idea. Not for closure. *Nein.* She just needs to stop avoiding the place.

Garages come and go. Mrs. Dolman with her children, the Dolmanites, bustle in and out of their front doors. Further along, Sal Perry's kids carry sodas while pedalling about in large plastic jeeps, and a childhood full of ice cream is delivered by chiming trucks. Schuld makes two quick rights up a lopsided tarmac driveway, hops off the skateboard, and enters the back gate at her place.

Panic pinches in her chest, and she thinks of curtains mauling windowsills, and of tarred plastic and bird feathers on beaches stuck to people's bare feet.

Turning away from bright noise, she can't stop thinking about death.

* * *

5:25 p.m. Schuld stares at water draining slowly from a clogged bathroom sink. She's unclear where the barking is coming from. It's behind her ears. It itches her skin.

Several minutes pass before the water drains to a grimy brown ring. Then she sits down on the toilet seat, drops solvent on a cleaning rod, picks up the semi-automatic handgun, and soaks the inside of the barrel.

4 Days to Wedding

<u>7:26 a.m.</u> P.J. stares at a ring of grime in the bathroom sink and worries about Kerstin's response if he doesn't clean it out. He puts on plastic gloves—in case she catches him in the bathroom without the appropriate handwear—before dousing it with bleach. Then he scrubs away with a cloth.

Kerstin takes his thoughts, and the more he goes into questions about them, the less stable everything becomes. This is how it feels around Pop, and the only way to get clear of it was to snort lines of coke. Otherwise, he spirals for days in a panic while he tries to make sure nothing around him is out of place. Is the apartment tidy? Are his clothes washed? Did he use mouthwash? Has he paid his bills and returned all his calls? He doesn't like that he has to be on top of it all, but once started, he can't stop.

P.J. rinses suds from the tub before he returns the bleach beneath the sink. Then he examines his handiwork to make certain there's no evidence of imperfection to be used against him. For the love of God, the movie date was a disaster. He shouldn't have mentioned the Navajo panties, and it was a huge mistake to rush into lovemaking so soon after a disagreement with Kerstin. If he could do it all again, he'd tell her what was bugging him (his visit with his father). However, he didn't know what to say about it exactly. He stares into the mirror to see if there's anything more that Kerstin can hold against him. First he straightens his collar. Then he wipes away a dab of toothpaste on his upper lip. There are too many pitfalls that could lead to her disapproval, so he washes his face again to ensure he hasn't overlooked anything that would give her another reason to get upset with him.

* * *

8:19 a.m. Kerstin, P. J., and Schuld smile at one another over breakfast, trying to stay one step ahead of each other. P.J. pushes the salt toward Kerstin in anticipation of her need to use it on her boiled eggs. She pushes it back to show it's not what she wants (and if she really wants it, she'll get it herself). Schuld is careful to scoop runny yolk onto her spoon and places it carefully in her mouth so it doesn't dribble down her chin.

"Feeling better today, Schuld?" P.J. asks.

"Yup," she replies.

"Stay away from your skateboard, darling," Kerstin says. "You don't want to push yourself too soon."

"Don't worry," she replies. "I won't sprain my wrists and jeopardize my ring-bearer duties."

"You're my priority," she says.

"Sure, Mutti," Schuld replies.

Kerstin's exhausted from worrying all the time about Schuld's strangeness. She goes God-knows-where with Woloff, and from what Kerstin can tell, she seems to have started listening to police scanners on the computer. Schuld told her she got a resumé out for an internship at the zoo and that no one got back to her. However, when Kerstin checked with her friend Laura, who works there, she found no one had seen an application from her. Schuld's becoming a lot like her father, who said all the right words but with little follow-through. What bullshit! People have got to mean what they say and say what they mean.

"How's the article coming along?" P.J. asks.

"Good," Kerstin replies. "I've got a bunch more research to do today if I'm going to meet tomorrow's deadline." She points to a ketchup stain on P.J.'s shirtsleeve. "You'll have to change that," she says.

"Thanks," he says. "I'll do it before I leave for my dentist appointment."

"Don't forget," she replies.

"I won't forget."

"You'd forget your arm if it wasn't attached to your body," she says.

"Of course I'd remember my arm!" he snaps.

"Geezus," she says.

The family gets quiet. Percolating. Regrouping. Smiling.

* * *

9:38 a.m. P.J. doesn't have to go to the dentist. Instead, he stops his car beside a light where Frankie, Pop's admin assistant, waits in an orange dress. He leans across the passenger seat to open the door, and she hops in.

"I got a copy of an internal memo Kerstin might find interesting for her article on the dead horses." She taps red nails on a beige folder while P.J. swerves into a steady stream of lunch-hour traffic. "Your father owns Copax Ltd., a subsidiary company that siphons blood from pregnant mares for eCG to sell to breeders trying produce farm animals like pigs efficiently."

"I don't follow," he replies as the car inches forward in a line that burps exhaust fumes.

"Pregnant horses are being drained of blood for much too long," she says. "They get anemia, but the company doesn't care. They want to increase their profits. So they keep doing it. Some of those poor horses died from kidney failure and have been dumped at random locations on the island."

"Fuck!" He waves to allow a car to enter the road from a side street. "Does Pop know about this?"

"Yup," she replies. "Take a look at the copies in the Copax Ltd. file. It's all there. Memos. Documents. Receipts. There have been twenty-six other deaths. Some of them miscarried foals."

The line of cars jilts forward, and P.J. accelerates to keep up with the surge of momentum.

"How is this happening without anyone knowing about it?"

"Confidentiality agreements are pretty strict, so there aren't that many people in the loop." They pass a huge hardware store that recently displaced small restaurants and clothing shops. "But I've been your father's admin assistant for so long, there isn't much that I don't get wind of."

"They're killing foals so people can have more hot dogs and bacon."

"This makes me sick to my stomach," she replies.

"Thanks for letting me know," P.J. says.

When they turn right at the corner beside a gas station, they enter a road that leads to fields of nothing but weeds spreading as far as the eye can see, a tangled carpet of crawling tentacles that clutch on to anything they can squeeze the shit out of.

* * *

10:21 a.m. After dropping Frankie off, P.J. drives to the closest convenience store for a pack of smokes. He's jumpy as he requests some Marlboros.

"Will there be anything else, sir?" the cashier asks him after money has been exchanged.

P.J. points to an ad beside the cash register. "It says, if you don't ask me if I'd like a Snickers bar with my purchase, I get one free."

The cashier clucks, irritated.

"Can I get my free Snickers?" P.J. asks.

"That deal expired at eight today," the cashier replies.

P.J. looks closely at an ad. "Gimme a break. It's been less than two hours."

"Two and a half hours," the cashier corrects.

"Give me the damn Snickers bar," P.J. says.

"Chillax, man."

"Don't be an asshole."

"You're the one who's being a jerk," the cashier replies.

"There are important distinctions between obeying the rules and interpreting them," P.J. yells. "Can't you be flexible?"

"There's no more deal, sir."

Once behind the steering wheel, P.J.'s hands quiver, and his heart thrashes against his rib cage. He drives onto the F-3 and accelerates until the pedal hits the floor. He takes a corner much too fast, and he only begins to slow down once he realizes he's driving one hundred kilometres per hour over the speed limit.

* * *

<u>10:22 a.m.</u> Back at the *Multi-modalZine*'s office, Kerstin stares at the contents of her spam folder and sees an advertisement for the church she's getting married in (they'll be expanding to include in their marriage package a swim with sharks— part of mandatory group counselling that incorporates psychological tests to chart compatibility). Even if Mutter is right about P.J., Kerstin can't back out of it with days to go. For crying out loud, everything is done already. One hundred and fifty-six guests have RSVP'd. Friends of her father have flown in from as far as Wales. There's a dress that's been paid for on her credit card and a registry with gifts that people have already purchased. It took a nasty argument with P.J. before a decision was made on the hall to hold the wedding reception, and they now have a terrific place to move into in a few months. She needs to own her choices, not sabotage them with thoughts that are fuelled by the stress of writing an article right before a huge life-changing event.

She moves into greater responsibility and calls Pop at his home office.

"Sorry to bother you, Mr. Banner," she says.

"No bother, Kerstin," he replies. "How can I help you today?"

"I just want to thank you for letting P.J. and me rent your beach house in Granger's Grove," she says. "You're a saint. This is such a godsend."

"I don't understand," he replies.

Kerstin repeats herself.

"There must be some miscommunication here, Kerstin," P.J. Sr. says. "I said no to Junior. I made it perfectly clear that I think you're both moving too fast, and that he needs to focus on his sobriety."

Kerstin is stunned. "I see," she replies.

"It's nothing personal," he says. "Junior has always depended on me for money, but he's forty-three now and talking about opening a studio without a steady list of clientele. This is a recipe for disaster, and I don't think he's thought through how he'll avoid leaning on you to make ends meet."

"I've got to go," Kerstin replies.

"Okay," P.J. Sr. replies.

On hanging up, she watches a black moth alight on the screen of the office window, its shadow casting gloom. Doom. She phones her father, and it goes to voice mail. Her stomach distends with nausea. Debris gathers in the bottom of her skull. She closes her eyes, hates what is happening to her, and doesn't give a damn if she goes to sleep and never wakes up again. Nothing unravels like the beautiful mind losing traces of the places it's been, she thinks.

Kerstin turns on her computer to look for apartment vacancies near the beach and sees a trending story on her screen.

ColinRiverdale@ColinRiverdale—8m
Real talk. Unbelievable. Geriatric Gerhard has a transvestite granddaughter. WHY ARE WE ONLY HEARING ABOUT THIS NOW?!!!!! This is more dishonesty from a man who lied to the voters about his contacts with the criminal Iqba Land Council. Just saying.

* * *

5:40 p.m. P.J. isn't ready for the scene unfolding in the lobby at Aspen Towers. Adrian casually stands by, working gum while his two men in judo uniforms chase Gee up the stairs with aluminum bats in hand.

"What the hell?" P.J shouts.

Adrian ignores him.

P.J. climbs the stairs three at a time. He hears the occasional whack, and Gee's muffled screams. His thighs burn, he's out of breath, and by the time he gets to the fourth floor, the men are walking back down the stairs.

"Stay the fuck up out of Adrian's business," one of the men says to him on passing by.

P.J. finds Gee slumped over in an open door to the roof. Panicked, he bends over him and stares down at a face that is a mound of bloody pulp.

"I give up," Gee mutters.

P.J. hoists him into a sitting position, takes off his shirt, and holds it over a flap of skin hanging open at the side of his face. "We need to get you to a hospital."

* * *

9:25 p.m. The courtyard in front of the Glass Hotel rasps with heat, the ground is lumpy with stone laid a hundred years ago, and a whirling spray of water surges from the fountain. Stomachs grumble among lovers sitting on steps in front of the spouting fountain, and there's not enough that can be done in the given amount of time.

Schuld releases tension on the dance floor in the Sickle Moon. Hopped up on marketable soul, she still hasn't heard about the tweet and shakes a leg while taking in the layout of the room. Four bouncers at the front door. A coat check. One dance floor. A bar. Booths with low tables. Stools. Toilets at the back. Two side exits.

Gyah!

Her neck is tight at the upper spine, so she closes her eyes and takes her shoulders for a stroll, rolling them to get rid of tension that pools in her upper back.

If she keeps her thoughts jammed with the right frequencies, she'll be able to keep choosing what ideas she lets in.

The club skips with ghetto funk, fa sho, and she puts her hips through some roller boogie. Then she goes off, cutting across the floor with scissor kicks inside squirts of glitter that cascade in bumplumpy strobe light. An Auto-Tuned voice sings in winks about *soixante-neuf* a mile high in the sky. Around her, nightclubbers step to beats in clumps of three or four, whooping and giddying up while DJ Lazlo shoots water with plastic guns onto the dance floor.

In the place to be, Schuld bops shoulders like a sex machine, whut!

* * *

9.47 p.m. Schuld and Woloff yak at the bar.

"Suffering is beyond what can be processed without sleep," she says to him. "And half the people in this club are out of their goddamn minds cuz they haven't had any rest." It's humid, and her innards yip with bad feelings.

"Wanna know something weird?" Woloff asks.

"Uh-huh," Schuld replies.

"Stars age backwards," Woloff says.

A buh-beat bumps, and they head out to the dance floor to

groove among other revellers. Not much is left in the tank, only enough to get through the mix where the house music gets crazy funky, and a fader ramps up in screeches. They both shake a leg among stacks of big hair and stupid optimism, like hanging sheets that toss about in a skyline of quaking teal.

And off they boom, moving to grooves that groom the ones who preen for the market. There's a smattering of shout-outs on the music track that they lap up like kitty-cats. In cascades of glitter—and plenty of it—they shake their shoulders, banging against the beat. Together, they take their hips for a stroll, sweet and insistent as a puffy crush of horns bend strobe light. Schuld throws her arms around Woloff's neck, everyone around them twerking. Twerk. Twerk. Sonic boom-booms, hopped-up faders jump the shark at one too many scratches, and then they bob to the poison that fills their heads: yummy like a shaking cymbal dangling in a holster.

Schuld clutches Woloff by the arm. "That's him," she shouts in his ear.

"Who?" he shouts back.

"The guy who broke my arm," she says.

"Where?"

She points at a bearded man with the bulbous belly of a linebacker. "Lame motherfucker," she says.

"Let's leave," Woloff replies.

"I'm not going anywhere," she says.

DJ Lazlo lays into a cello banging the shit out of the sound system as Schuld quickly moves off among falling balloons and frilly decorations. When she reaches the man's table, she leans forward and yells in his bearded face. He stands, shoving her hard. She pushes back. He grabs her shoulder and wrestles her to the floor. Schuld knees him in the gut before pushing him off her, her gun falling out of her waistband. He reaches for it, but she's quicker. Quick. Everything turns quickly as she squeezes the trigger.

Pop.

The bullet lands harmlessly in a floorboard, and the man scrambles to his feet and makes a run for it into the crowd of people storming exits. Schuld's vaguely aware of Woloff clutching on to her by the collar and pulling her past upturned tables in the direction of his motorbike. He pushes open the back door, and they dip into an alley.

"I almost shot him," she says.

He undoes the chain lock and climbs onto his bike. "It was an accident."

"That's sure as shit not gonna matter."

"We've gotta get out of here," Woloff replies.

Schuld jumps on and wraps her arms around his waist before they speed toward the F-3, clipping weeds overhanging the road.

How much damage has she done? She doesn't know for sure, but she no longer wants to be at the centre of human affairs.

A gust of wind rattles her. She retches on the road, uncertain what story she's been misplaced in.

Woloff drives past batches of dried flowers wrapped around lampposts to remember the dead. Up ahead, traffic slows where a platoon of soldiers in haz-mat suits blowtorch the tumbling foliage. The heat intensifies as the motorbike approaches them.

He accelerates, pulling behind a van that is going to make it across the road before the fire does. They can feel the flush of heat, the rush of it making them flinch as they drive into wisps of smoke.

* * *

<u>9:58 p.m.</u> Kerstin pounces as soon as P.J. walks through the front door. "Have you seen Schuld?" she asks. "I've been leaving messages, but her phone isn't on."

"No." He has spent the past three hours at the emergency, and he's dazed. "Did something happen?"

"There was a tweet from Colin Riverdale that outed her online."

"Dear God." He remembers telling Pop about Schuld. Up until this morning, he never would have thought Pop capable of using it to get his land deal. "Did you try the gallery?"

"She wasn't there either."

It had to be him. "If you've got Woloff's address, I could see if she's there."

She stands in the hallway, blocking his way into the living room. "When were you going to tell me about the beach house?" she asks.

"What are you talking about?" he replies, placing a beige file on a dresser beside the door.

"I spoke to your father today," she says.

P.J. feels pressure in his bladder, shuffles from foot to foot, and tries to think of a way out of the mess he's created for himself. "I was embarrassed."

Kerstin sticks a finger in his chest. "You're a liar," she says.

"I didn't want to disappoint you," he replies.

"Would you stop with the bullshit?" Kerstin catches hold of his wrist and twists tight. "This isn't my fault."

He tries to pry her fingers loose.

"What else are you lying about?" She digs her nails into his skin. "Did you just freebase coke?" She grabs at the lapel of his shirt with her hand. "Are you fucking someone else?"

"No," he says.

"Liar!"

"Just take a look in the file," he says.

"Go peddle your bullshit somewhere else," she replies. "I've got enough to worry about with Schuld." She pushes him hard, and he falls backwards against the dresser.

Everything tumbles to the floor, and he lies in a heap among the contents of the beige folder strewn around him.

"Go!"

He sits up, breathing heavily. "Kerstin, just take a look at the documents."

"Get out."

He gathers papers scattered on the floor and holds a sheet up to her. "Pop has people bleeding horses for eCG at Copax Ltd. That's how they died."

As P.J. gets to his feet, she smells urine and sees a wet patch on the front of his trousers "You're shaking," she says.

"Please take a look," he implores. "Please, Kerstin. Please."

"Are you okay?"

His eyes brim with tears. "Please."

"Your hands are—"

"Please."

"Alright." She takes the file out of his hand. "Sit for a moment."

"I'm good," he replies.

He watches her read.

"Do you have originals?" she asks.

"Copies."

"Can you get originals?"

"Not of these. No."

"We need originals," she says. "These could be forged by anyone."

"Are you saying Pop's going to get away with it?" he asks.

Before she can respond, they're interrupted by a knock at the front door.

"Police!" a voice says.

P.J. brushes himself off while Kerstin opens up to a uniformed police officer, a woman with a purple, heart-shaped birthmark on her cheek.

"We're looking for Phillip Ostheim in connection with a shooting at a nightclub," the cop says.

"What are you saying?" Kerstin asks.

"We have video footage of him fleeing the scene on a motorcycle," he says.

"She's not here," P.J. replies.

"So you won't mind if we look around," the cop says.

Kerstin steps back with the beige file of unusable photocopies shaking in her quaking hand.

3 Days to Wedding

<u>12:04 a.m.</u> Undone by attachments to ideas she thought possible, Schuld climbs with Woloff the rungs of a metal ladder attached to the side of a bleached brick tower mill on the spur of a hill outside Ogweyo's Cove. Their belly muscles ache. Their rib cages and costosternal bones in their chests feel embedded with shards of glass. They grit teeth, pull themselves up, and focus on a metal platform below the windmill's circling iron blades. Schuld hoists herself onto the ice-cold metal platform, steps up to an entranceway, and waits for Woloff to join her before they both lean hard against a plywood board.

Nothing.

They hitch their hips, straining against screws.

It's pointless.

Their lungs, famished linings, crackle among static hisses in a drooped overhang of electric wires.

Mosquitoes flick against their teeth as they charge the plywood board. The moon dangles in gibbering atoms.

* * *

<u>3:06 a.m.</u> They sit cross-legged on flattened cardboard in front of a rotating capstan wheel. They grit their teeth as embers of sadness burn in their guts. Cockroaches scuttle among wooden beams beneath the ceiling, and they occasionally stare up at the sound of beetles randomly hitting the window.

Everything they thought is really quite wrong.

Fish with bioluminescent organs from abyssal depths have made it onto the shore, their gill legs dragging their bellies along the sand before waves rush in, without notice, to carry them back into the ocean. Ovaries sprout as fruit on trees. Seeds grow limbs. Stones, mountains, and bodies of water shape-shift at will while death lurks in parts that leave fissures between thoughts that command and bodies that refuse to obey. There's no stable foundation to build a life on, only a chaotic swirl that expresses itself in nonsensical blather.

"It was an accident," Woloff says. "You can beat the charge."

"You'd think," Schuld says.

"Nobody got hurt."

"Will it matter?" she replies.

Sirens bray downwind between the present and future perfect, and out of place in the sensible order of things they hate for real.

* * *

<u>5:19 a.m.</u> As Schuld and Woloff pace up and down in the tower mill, they don't quite feel like themselves. They don't know what to do, so they jump up and down, unsaying in fits that won't adapt. They work up a sweat, leaping higher and

234

higher until they unbecome, the bowls of their minds filling with mist. Then they crouch low together at the windowsill to stare, out of breath, through bars at weeds taking over a macadamia nut plantation.

Orange cones are scattered among potholes and old tractor parts among banana trees crawling with bougainvilleas. Scattered pools of oil slick the broken tarmac road bordered by mustard flowers. In the middle of the field, a chimney stack caked in rust teeters on a foundation of red bricks beside a solar panel on a pole.

They sit, leaning against the wall. Then they measure ways they've split with the outside world to build an island on their backs, and they imagine utopias among rainbow trees. Mice scurry by their feet, and near their ears. Their dingle/ rattle only stopping when they consider the end date: curtains, and their misguided hope they'd be remembered in a reading of their eulogy by how they inspired a generation to take up the anti-hero's pilgrimage outside history.

Doubt licks at Woloff's inner ear, an iguana tongue darting right, maybe left. Why did she bring the gun? Schuld tries to explain, but it doesn't seem right to put into words, as if trying to do so leaves only her talking head analyzing, after the fact. She wishes to cinch her wrist, twist. Then release. Woloff thinks of Namunyuk, her inability to see anything in his future. Roughage tumbles hard with grit in his stomach like a panicked flamboyance of flamingos.

Tic toc.

They crinkle up cellophane paper and feel like figures that soldier through trace intensities of smashed colour. There's clanging in their brains. Geezus, does it matter whether the lights flickering on the edge of the panorama take place in their eyes or in the hut of their heads? Stinkbugs crawl along their forearms. Sleeplessness threatens to pull them under. Then it hits them all at once—and there's all this space to lie out in—fatigue has been talking for some time now.

Juddering to their feet, they hold it together beneath a light bulb swinging willy-nilly on a cord. They push open the plywood door and step onto the platform under the windmill's circling blades. Unwilling to lose their attachment to a possible future, they kiss before clambering down the ladder that hangs among transmission lines blathering with repeating code.

One Year Later

<u>9:10 p.m.</u> P.J. and Kerstin stretch out on a woollen blanket near the foot of the sand cliffs at Ka'alipo Beach. They stare up at all that they can't see going on in the entire universe and think of how scribbles of galaxies draw attention to the ways future generations will wonder, what the fuck? Kicked-up wind infolds around them. They squeeze closer for warmth, plundered by desires that herd them into bottomless seriousness despite those who misunderstand the choices they've made together.

"You see Orion?" P.J. points to a trio of stars that make up the hunter's belt.

"It's the only one I can make out," Kerstin replies.

"I can't tell which ones are supposed to be his dogs."

"There." She points. "See?"

"*Nein.*"

"*Nein?*"

"*Nein.*"

She stamps out a butt, takes him by the hand, and he follows her behind a saltbush. Then she pulls him down into the beach grass, her hand working fingers on skin beneath his jacket. He flips up her pale-blue wedding dress, finding her hip, in the glow of a blood moon.

P.J. looks.

Her bra strap hangs off her shoulder. Close up, her hair is a nest of loose frosty curls parted left, and a nose that drops above that pink mouth she once claimed was overfull with tongue.

He takes her nipple in his mouth and plays it between his lips. Spreading her legs, she watches him tug off her underwear and drop down to kiss her inner thighs.

Her ringed fingers gripping the earth, she opens her legs wider, and they're pulled someplace they can't name with any accuracy.

Captive to conscious stirrings, her hands wrap around his head. An eruption of solar flares rip through the stratosphere and they budge just a little bit more into damage with consequences to unpack, hoping to learn ways to live without equilibrium after being pressed, for so long, up against all that rage over Pop. Sky heaves. Laughter rises from behind another bush, and they both feel slightly panicked at how silly they've been for not seeing there isn't anything to do except care for each other now.

* * *

11:03 p.m. Kerstin and P.J stand on the sand facing one another. They hold hands, time congeals, and, overshooting its mark, the ocean water spreads up their bare feet as they share their vows.

Air caterwauls with the smell of sea salt, and on the west side of the island, Schuld and Woloff sit on the garden patio of their rented cottage. Violet flowers spread up a bannister, bringing with them mosquitoes that nibble on their skin. Gravity drags dust to dusk. The earth tilts on its wobbly axis. Hoping for little, more or less, they make the moment matter by unhurriedly watching the caterpillars spin silky cocoons in trees.

It smells like stars.

Acknowledgements

In writing this manuscript, I have benefited greatly from the close readings, suggestions, insights, and support of a large number of people. I express my gratitude to Carmen Nolte-Odhiambo, Paul Lyons, Malcolm Sutton, Jay Millar and Hazel Millar at Book*hug, Jennifer Lyons, Kai Cheng Thom, Mark Helbling, Stephen Canham, Craig D. Howes, Gary Pak, Laura Lyons, Joan Peters, Jack Taylor, Anna Feuerstein, M. Thomas Gammarino, George Elliott Clarke, Amy Nishimura, my fine colleagues at University of Hawai'i—West O'ahu, Barack Odhiambo, Florence Odhiambo, Birgit Nolte, Claus Nolte, and Momo and Teo. I also thank the Canada Council for the Arts for financial assistance provided for this project.

D. Nandi Odhiambo is the author of three novels: *diss/ed banded nations* (1998), *Kipligat's Chance* (2003), and *The Reverend's Apprentice* (2008). Originally from Nairobi, Kenya, Nandi moved to Winnipeg, Manitoba, in the 1970s. He has an MFA in creative writing from the University of Massachusetts, Amherst, and a PhD in English from the University of Hawai'i, Manoa. Currently Nandi lives in O'ahu, Hawai'i, with his wife Carmen and two dogs, where he works as an Assistant Professor of English at the University of Hawai'i, West O'ahu.

Colophon

Distributed in Canada by the Literary Press Group:
www.lpg.ca

Shop online at www.bookthug.ca

Designed by Malcolm Sutton
Edited for the press by Malcolm Sutton
Copy-edited by Stuart Ross

BOOK
PRODUCTION
WAR ECONOMY
STANDARD